A Lock of Silver Hair

(Book 7: An Irish Family Saga)

by

Jean Reinhardt

Historical Fiction

Every old man I see
In October-coloured weather
Seems to say to me:
"I was once your father."

From the poem 'Memory of my Father' by

Patrick Kavanagh

(Born in county Monaghan)

DEDICATION

This book is dedicated to my father

Jack Parker.

(1933-2017)

A NOTE FROM THE AUTHOR

This is probably the last novella in the series but at some time in the future I may write a stand-alone book about a few of the characters that I've grown to love in this saga. It has taken me a long time to finish this one and I struggled to bring it to a conclusion, mostly due to the fact that my father died while I was two thirds of the way through it. When you read it you will understand why this was so difficult for me.

I want to thank you, the reader, for your support and the interest you've taken in my writing. It really encourages me to keep going and I feel blessed to have been able to fulfil a lifelong ambition. I have wanted to write a book since my teenage years but never even considered the fact that I might write more than one, or that it was possible for me to make any sort of a living from being an author.

At the moment, I'm working on a novel set at the end of the First World War, inspired by a granduncle from my side of the family and one from my husband's. Both of these men died very young, at twenty and twenty-one, but I wanted to add some more years to their lives and came up with a fictional storyline where they would meet up and become friends. It will take me the best part of a year to write this one, but if you're interested in reading it, please send an email to me at; *jeanreinhardt@yahoo.co.uk* and I will let you know as soon as it's ready for publishing.

McGrother Family Tree

Pat and Annie McGrother: James's uncle and aunt.

Maggie: James's older widowed sister.

James McGrother married Mary Roarke (1845)
They had 5 children: Catherine, Thomas, Mary-Anne, Breege and Jamie.

Catherine married Patrick Gallagher (1866)
They had 3 children: Tom (Dr. Gilmore's Son), Maisie and Ellen.

Thomas's first wife was Jane (she died young).
They had 1 child: Eliza.
His second wife was Lily.
They had 1 child: Jeremiah (adopted).

Mary-Anne married Sergeant Broderick.
They had 1 child: George (Dr. Gilmore's son by a servant girl, adopted by Mary-Anne).

Breege was single with no children.

Jamie married Annie.
They had two daughters and two sons.

Francis McGrother was a cousin of James's, transported to Australia in the mid 1800's for stealing a cow.

Frank McGrother was born and reared in Australia, the youngest of Francis McGrother's four sons.

(This is a fictional family tree but it contains some actual ancestors of the author).

CHAPTER ONE

The beams of moonlight filtering through the trees would have been a welcome sight to anyone making their way through thick woodland in the dead of night. To the four men hiding behind a tangle of brambles it was the reason for them being there, lying chilled to the bone, inert as corpses.

Jamie McGrother held his breath, listening intently to every sound coming from the surrounding woodland. His companions were doing likewise and if their circumstances had been different it would have been one of those sublime moments to be savoured and memorized, as a favourite painting might be to an admirer of the arts.

Thirty cold, nerve-wrecking minutes went by before anyone dared to move or make the slightest sound.

"That was close, lads," Jamie whispered, "Too close."

"They must have believed Broderick," one of the men remarked.

"I think you mean *Sergeant* Broderick," corrected Jamie. "It's his English accent that fools them, works every time. We'll have to start practising it ourselves."

He raised a hand and held his breath, listening one more time to the silence surrounding them.

"It's safe enough to carry on now, lads. I reckon those militiamen are so far away, Fergus could take off his boots and they still wouldn't find us," Jamie nudged his brother-in-law crouching next to him.

"Your own feet don't smell so sweet," was the response.

The men stood up and stretched their cramped legs, rubbing some warmth back into them. They continued to speak in hushed tones, not fully convinced a safe enough distance lay between them and the militia that had been hot on their heels before the sergeant came along on his bike to divert them.

The diversion had been part of the plan, should anything go wrong. Reeking of alcohol, he wobbled along the hedgerows on his bicycle like an old drunk with just enough control of his balance to avoid landing in the ditch. In this beguiling state of intoxication, Sergeant Broderick called out to the militia, demanding they arrest those 'scoundrels' that knocked him off his bike. When asked which direction they had taken, he sent the armed men down a track that would lead them far away from the field Jamie and his companions had raced across on their way towards the forest.

"Is it safe enough to smoke yet?" Fergus held an unlit cigarette between his shivering lips.

"I reckon it is," Jamie replied. "You're shaking like a leaf, it's not that cold. You farmers are a very soft breed, altogether. Or have your nerves gotten the better of you?"

Fergus snorted, used to being ribbed over his aversion to cold weather, "Can I help it if I'm a hot blooded man. Anyways, you fishermen are as cold as your catch. You'd melt in a bit of sunshine."

The friendly mocking continued, and once the cigarettes had been lit and inhaled deeply to calm their nerves, the men discussed their next move. It was agreed the youngest two should go to a house where a regular card game took place. It was a good alibi and the other players would vouch for them. Jamie and Fergus watched until they disappeared into the shadows before starting out on their own journey. Although the danger of being caught seemed to have passed, the men kept a watchful eye and a keen ear alert for any sign of being followed.

"Us older men need to stick together, eh, Jamie?" Fergus matched his companion's steady pace, thankful for the warmth returning to his body.

"I would much prefer to take my chances alone, Fergus. But I promised Annie I'd stick close to her brother and she could make life miserable for me if she found out we had separated."

"Well, I won't be the one to tell her, if you'd like to carry on without me."

Although Jamie was sure his brother-in-law had not been insulted by his remark, he detected a slight edge to the other man's voice.

"I didn't mean you would hinder me in any way, Fergus. You know yourself that a man on his own has less chance of being found. Common sense, that's all it is."

"I know, Jamie. I know. I would be happier if you didn't tell Annie about our little *adventures*, though. What she doesn't know, she cannot tell – isn't that what they say?"

"What your sister doesn't know she'll find out, by hook or by crook. It's best she is prepared for any knocks that might come to her door in the middle of the night. Annie will say I am helping you find a missing sheep but if we continue to stroll along at this snail's pace, the ewe will get fed up waiting and find her own way home."

Fergus punched Jamie in the shoulder and laughed. As they picked up speed, he pointed to the night sky, visible through the overhead branches.

"I thought we were to have the cover of thick cloud for our mission. Did you not say there was a storm due in from the east?" he remarked.

"You can't blame me for the weather, Fergus. Sure that's why there was no fishing tonight – on account of the storm."

"Well, it's as calm as a sleeping child, Jamie. A perfect night for fishing, I'd say."

The men paused at the edge of the woodland, their eyes scanning a large moonlit field they were to cross.

"Only a farmer would say such a thing," Jamie replied, stepping out from the shelter of the trees.

Before they were even halfway across, clouds rushed in to darken the sky and by the time they reached the other side they were soaked to the skin.

"There's your storm, Fergus," gloated Jamie, cold and wet but vindicated.

CHAPTER TWO

James sat in his chair by the fire in Paddy Mac's, ignoring the sideward glances of the proprietor standing behind the counter. Johnny MacMahon had returned from America and taken over the business when his father, known to everyone as Paddy Mac, had died. Although Paddy's son had been called Johnny Mac since his childhood, he kept the original name over the door. He knew that even if he replaced it, the pub would always be referred to as Paddy Mac's. Moreover, he found it comforting to hear his father's name still mentioned so often, long after he had died.

The place was almost empty except for two men sitting at the bar. They had been deep in conversation when James walked in but paused to greet him. His stiff nod in return told them he was not in a talkative mood.

Often his son, Jamie, accompanied him and the time spent together, even in silent contemplation, was always special. His youngest was a busy man, with a wife and four young children to provide for. Between fishing and labouring, and some activities James did not approve of, there was never enough time in the day for Jamie.

For the first twelve months after his mother's death Jamie had not let his father out of his sight, and when he couldn't watch him he had half the village doing it for him. The whole parish knew that not a drop of whiskey had passed James McGrother's lips in the last few years. Even the porter he allowed himself three times in the week was carefully measured out in slow, deliberate sips, making two pints of it last for the evening.

James knew of his son's concern and, although it irritated him at first, he never objected to being accompanied by him whenever he ventured into one of his two favourite watering holes. In time, the feeling of being watched was replaced by the pleasure of his son's company and the two men had grown even closer because of it. Eventually, Jamie stopped worrying that his father might seek comfort from a whiskey bottle.

James kept his eye on the door, knowing his son would walk through it at any minute. Johnny Mac had been surprised at the request for a whiskey instead of the usual porter but knew better than to question his customer's choice of drink. Instead, he sent his wife out to warn James's family about the glass of spirit sitting within arm's reach of him.

This had not gone unnoticed by James and when his eye wasn't on the whiskey, it was on the door. Sure enough, within ten minutes of Johnny's wife leaving the premises, one of the McGrothers appeared. Jamie nodded a cursory greeting to the men at the bar as he strode across the scuffed, wooden floor. Pulling a chair out from the table to sit opposite his father, he tried to keep his eyes from wandering to the glass sitting between them.

"Will I get you a porter, Da? I'm having one myself."

James could see the anxieties of life etched into his son's face and his conscience stabbed at him for adding to his worries. He knew only too well the heavy weight of responsibility resting on Jamie's shoulders. It had never been his intention to add to that burden and it was at times like this the reality of his situation hit him, like the sharp sting of a schoolmaster's cane across the knuckles of a day-dreaming pupil.

"Were you mending the nets, son?" asked James.

"I was, Da. Would you not come with me and give us a hand? I could do with the help."

James leaned forward and pushed the glass across the table. "Here, drink this before I give in to temptation," he said.

The whiskey disappeared in one gulp and Jamie felt a warm tingle as it sank into his empty stomach. With the temptation out of the way, a sense of relief settled over the young man and he raised his hand towards the bar to order the promised porter for his father.

"Put your hand down, son. We'll not be staying," James reached inside his jacket and removed a piece of paper. "There's bad news from America and you know how quickly that can spread when it comes in the form of a telegram."

As he took the paper from his father's trembling fingers, Jamie felt a chill in the pit of his stomach, in spite of the whiskey he had just put there. He stared at the words leaping out at him and blinked repeatedly, as if the action would somehow change their meaning.

"He's dead?" a stunned Jamie looked up at his father.

James leaned forward to bury his face in weathered, old hands. Hearing the words spoken aloud made the reality of the message sink in. The pain shooting through him could not have been more intense had it been caused by the knife he used for gutting fish.

"Are you ailing, James?" Johnny Mac was standing behind Jamie's chair. Neither of the men answered him. "Is it bad news you're after getting?"

James wiped his face with his palms before looking up. He saw that his son was still staring in disbelief at the telegram and reached across to take it from him, but Jamie crumpled it into a tight ball. He aimed it at the fireplace then stood up and took his father by the arm.

"Come on, Da. We had best get over to Mary-Anne before she hears this from one of the neighbours. I'm sorry, Johnny, you'll have to pardon our manners but I'm not able to speak about it. I don't think either of us are at the minute."

Jamie led his father from the premises, neither of them uttering a word of explanation for their sudden departure. The ball of paper had landed on the hearth and Johnny Mac picked it up, conscious of the stares from the two men at the bar. As he unravelled it, a name stood out and he held his breath, hoping the news would not be as bad as he suspected. But it was.

CHAPTER THREE

It didn't take long for the sad news of Thomas McGrother's death to spread throughout the parish. By the time it was announced in the Dundalk Democrat, the whole of county Louth was aware of it. Letters of condolence came to James from various parts of the country and from his relatives in England, but it was the one written by Catherine on behalf of the family in New York that gave him the most comfort. In a separate envelope inside that letter was an unfinished one Thomas had intended sending to his father the week he died. James took it out of a wooden box under his bed and read it again, for the umpteenth time, his eyes drinking in every word written in his son's neat hand.

Dearest Da,

I hope this letter finds you in good health and good spirit. These past few days I find myself reminiscing on my Irish childhood and of the many times I ran barefoot over the bog, while you and Uncle Pat cut and footed the turf. You both should have been much stricter with me, making me do my fair share of the work. I know that my sweet Eliza has the same fond memories of her own early years and I'm truly grateful to you and Ma for giving her such a precious gift. No grandparents could have done more for a child and you filled my place as a father better than I could have ever done myself.

I may have been an absent parent where my daughter was concerned but that is not the case with my son. Jeremiah sticks to me like a limpet, and that is as it should be, is it not? Did I mention in a previous letter that we have bicycles now? We have even joined a wheelman club but your grandson finds it difficult to keep his speed below twelve miles to the hour, which is the limit on the special bicycle paths we regularly use.

Jeremiah's favourite place to visit is Coney Island. You would find it tiresome there, Da, the same way you do not relish the multitudes descending on Blackrock on August 15th for the Farmers' Holiday. Now imagine that crowd multiplied many times over. I absolutely refuse to accompany him in the summer season, when there is not an inch of space to be found anywhere.

In this regard, I am becoming more like you as I grow older and as soon as Jeremiah has completed his education I intend on moving out of the city to its more tranquil surrounding countryside. Lily will no doubt cause a fuss but the trains run frequently into New York from all directions now and a day trip would

Apparently, Lily had been calling Thomas to his supper and he placed the letter under a paperweight with the intention of finishing it the following evening. That never happened. He was badly injured while reporting on a riot that took place the following day and died of his wounds that night at the hospital.

In her letter, Catherine explained that Thomas had taken the place of a young reporter assigned to cover a riot erupting in the streets of the city. Her brother feared the young man was too inexperienced to handle such a volatile situation and called him back as he was about to leave. Thomas wouldn't even allow him to accompany him. The only witness to the fatal incident was a ten year old boy.

Catherine did not include every detail reported to the family by the police, not wanting to make the bad news she was delivering any more painful than necessary. So James was told that his son had been crushed in a rioting crowd, but what really happened was a different story altogether.

The young boy who witnessed Thomas's death had followed a group of irate men into an abandoned building. Thomas appeared and grabbed the child by the arm, pulling him back outside, away from any danger. Having scoured the premises the men caught sight of Thomas, and thinking he was up to no good with the struggling boy, they beat him to within an inch of his life. The frightened child ran in a panic through the streets, straight into a group of policemen, brandishing their billy clubs. Once they calmed him down, he led them to where Thomas lay unconscious in a pool of blood.

One of the policemen recognized the stricken man and volunteered to call to Lily with the bad news. At the hospital the family took turns by Thomas's bedside, praying for him to regain consciousness. Eliza had been sent for and was on her way immediately but her father died before she arrived, there being no direct railway link to New York City from Annapolis.

The pain of losing his wife had never left James. He gradually became accustomed to its presence until it felt more like a dull ache. The loss of his eldest son opened that wound again and his emotions were so raw, he thought his heart would give out. At least with Mary, James had been given time to prepare himself, which didn't lessen his grief but gave him the opportunity to bare his soul to her. He had felt closer to his wife in their last few weeks together than he had at any other time in their marriage, and he was sure it had been the same for Mary.

All the unspoken words James had meant to say to Thomas came flooding into his head, but it was too late now. He regretted the short letters he had rushed off in reply to his son's long, endearing missives, and berated himself for not spending more time over them, putting down on paper what was really in his heart. Did Thomas know how much his father loved him? How much he still missed him, even though he had left for America decades before? It was too late to tell him now and James was full of remorse over his fear of sounding too soft if he had done so in his letters.

Carefully folding the letters from Catherine and Thomas he thought about his youngest, Jamie. So many times, he had wanted him to know how much he meant to him, but held back. Men were not supposed to speak such things to each other, *'But why not?'* thought James. *'If a mother can open her heart to her daughter, surely a father can do likewise to his son?'*

It had always been easy for James to let his girls know how much he loved them but treating boys in the same manner was never encouraged, for fear of making them too soft.

James placed the letters under his pillow and lay down, worn out from grief. From now on, if he wanted to tell his son or grandsons he loved them, he would. Whether it was a quiet word in private or in a letter, James was determined to do so, no matter what convention dictated.

CHAPTER FOUR

The sound of quiet weeping stirred Annie from her sleep and she woke up to find herself alone in bed. A quick glance across to the other side of the room told her the sound was not coming from either of her two youngest children. A beam of moonlight lay across their sleeping faces, so Annie thought one of their daughters in the room below must have had a nightmare and assumed Jamie had gone down to comfort her. Although they shared a room with their grandfather, he was a sound sleeper and was rarely disturbed by any noise the children made.

When she sat up to listen more intently, Annie realized the weeping wasn't coming from the rear bedroom below. Although the door to their tiny room at the top of the stairs was shut tight, the muffled sobbing filtered through. Leaving her warm bed, Annie pulled a shawl around her shoulders before opening the door leading down to the kitchen.

Jamie was sitting in his chair by the stove, a shaft of moonlight falling across his bowed head and drooping shoulders.

"I'm sorry, love, I didn't mean to wake you," he held out his arms to his wife. "That's why I left the bedroom. I don't know what's come over me at all. I woke up and my face was wet with tears."

Annie sat on his knee, wrapping her shawl around them both. She hardly knew Thomas, her brother-in-law, what distressed her was witnessing the pain her husband and his father suffered because of their loss.

"Were you dreaming of your brother?" she asked.

Jamie shook his head, "I don't think I was dreaming of anything. But I must have been if I'm in this state now."

Annie kissed his wet cheek, just above the line of his beard. "You've been a tower of strength to your da, Jamie. It isn't easy to keep all that grief inside you."

"You're very fortunate, Annie. I envy you that all of your family are still around you. Not one of them has emigrated."

"Nor died," said Annie. "Except for grandparents, of course. I cannot imagine how painful it must be to lose a brother or a parent. Even when the boys go across the water for a bit of work during the winter, you would swear they had gone for good, I'm that upset about it," Annie sniffed back a welcome tear, "You have me as bad as yourself now," she said.

Jamie knew she was doing her best to empathize with the depth of his sadness and squeezed her hand.

"At least he hasn't taken to drowning his sorrows with the drink. That's a blessing in itself," he said.

"Who? Your da?"

Jamie nodded, "I was afraid he might when Maggie died so soon after Ma."

"Poor Aunt Maggie. That was hard on your Da, right enough. Losing his sister so quickly after he lost his wife," Annie sighed and shed a few more heartfelt tears. "The children miss them both something terrible."

They sat in silent contemplation for a long time, until the shaft of moonlight disappeared from the window. Eventually, with the cold air biting at their bare feet, the couple rose to return to the comfort of their bed. With Annie curled up beside him, asleep almost as soon as her head lay on his chest, Jamie counted his blessings as a second sleep of the night overtook him.

******

Far away from Blackrock, none of Jamie's family in New York had been counting their blessings. Lily admitted to Catherine that if it wasn't for her son Jeremiah, she would have readily followed Thomas to the grave. Some days she was inconsolable and Jeremiah would hear her weeping throughout the night. In the mornings he always checked to see what state she was in before deciding on whether or not he would attend college that day.

Concern for his mother took the edge from his own grief. He had suffered more than the loss of a parent with the death of his father; he had lost a good friend. Thomas's bicycle stood next to Jeremiah's in the hallway, a constant reminder of the precious time they spent together. Lily had wanted to give it away but relented when Jeremiah begged her not to. She was taken aback at how upset he became at the thought of not seeing it each time he returned home.

Having had a good night's sleep, for a change, Jeremiah woke early and listened outside his mother's door but not a sound could be heard. Not wanting to disturb her, he entered quietly without knocking and stood by her bed. The heavy curtains were drawn but even in the dim light he could see that she was sleeping peacefully and breathed a sigh of relief. He could attend college that day, as Catherine would be calling later in the morning.

Ellen was already awake and had returned from the bathroom shared by the four apartments on their floor. She put her ear to Lily's door as Jeremiah had done.

"I have just been in to see how she is, Ellen. She seems to be having a good sleep, do you think I should go to college today?" Jeremiah was sitting at the table.

His cousin Ellen, had been living with the family for the past few years and had gained employment as a full time teacher in a local parish school. Her income was needed even more so, now that Thomas was gone. She couldn't afford to miss any more days than she already had.

"I don't see why not, Jeremiah. Ma will be here in a few hours and I wouldn't be surprised if Lily was still asleep when she arrives," Ellen ruffled his hair. "Besides, you have missed enough lessons as it is, young man."

"Spoken like a true teacher," was his reply. "But I think I shall stay until Aunt Catherine arrives. Will you write me a note please, excusing me from this morning's lesson?"

After his cousin had left for work, Jeremiah fetched his satchel and took out some books to catch up on his studies. An hour later, he was so engrossed in his work he never heard Lily

25

come into the parlour and jumped when she laid a hand on his shoulder.

"I'm sorry, son. I didn't mean to startle you. Why did you not go to college this morning? Are you unwell?"

Jeremiah looked disconcertingly at his mother. Surely she realized that he was afraid to leave her alone in the state she had been in since his father died? But Lily stood there, drawing her shawl around her shoulders as she waited for an answer.

"I thought you might need me to fetch you something at the grocer's. You haven't left home since . . . since . . ." his voice trailed off.

"I know, son. I know," Lily nodded and squeezed his shoulder. "But Catherine will be here soon and no doubt she will have a week's worth of food with her, so there is no need for you to be missing your lessons. I slept all night and feel the better for it. I might even go out for a stroll later."

Jeremiah could see his mother was in good spirits so packed his books back into their satchel. She kissed him goodbye before returning to her bedroom to get dressed. His bicycle was resting against his father's and as he pulled it away, the handlebars became entangled. As he tried to wrench them free a wave of grief flooded through him and Jeremiah struggled to remain composed. He didn't want his mother to get upset again so called out to her that he was taking the tram instead.

By the time Lily came out to ask him why, he was gone. Her eyes were drawn to the two bicycles, their handlebars entwined, and Thomas came immediately to mind. She held her breath and waited for the stab of pain that always accompanied his memory but it didn't come. Instead, she felt strangely comforted and stared for some time at the interlocked handlebars, not wanting to let go of the sensation. It ended when three sharp raps on the door announced Catherine's arrival.

CHAPTER FIVE

"Da, are you awake?" Jamie's voice sounded very far away to his father.

"I am now," muttered James as he struggled to sit up. "Is the house on fire?"

When his son came closer to sit on the side of his bed James sensed an air of excitement about him. He glanced across the room to the bed his granddaughters shared, and saw it was empty. James raised an eyebrow as he waited for an explanation for being disturbed at such an early hour in the morning.

"You have a letter, Da, from Australia of all places. I think it's from your cousin, Francis McGrother," Jamie handed over the envelope. "I'll fetch you a cup of tea while you read it."

James saw the name F. McGrother written above the return address on the back of the envelope. Nobody in the family had heard anything from the young man who had been transported to Van Diemen's Land for stealing a cow, more than fifty years ago. For all anyone knew he could have died on the ship before he even got there.

When Jamie returned with a steaming cup of tea his father was still staring at the unopened envelope. The younger man couldn't blame him for his reluctance to read what was inside. Letters from abroad of late had contained nothing but bad news for the McGrother family in Blackrock.

"Shall I read it to you, Da? The light in here isn't so good."

Relieved, James handed over the envelope and sipped the hot sweet tea. "Is Annie about?" he asked.

"She has taken the children to school this morning. I was about to get into my bed when this arrived," Jamie's eyes swept over the neat script as he spoke.

"Did ye have a decent catch this time, son?"

"We did. It was the best night's fishing this week," Jamie looked up from the page he was quickly scanning. "This is from your cousin's son. He must be called after his father but he has signed it, Frank. He says;

'Dear Cousin James,

I hope this letter finds you in good health. No doubt you will be surprised to hear from your cousin's family on the other side of the world. I am sorry to have to tell you that my father Francis passed away last year after a long illness.'

Jamie stopped reading at the news of another death but his father urged him to continue.

'Although he made a good life for himself and his family, here in Australia, in his final months he became very homesick. My brothers and myself grew up listening to stories about his childhood in Monaghan and you were often mentioned in them. As he was the youngest in his family, he is sure that all of his brothers and sisters will have passed away by now and as far as he knows, you are his closest relative still living in Ireland and his best remembered childhood friend.

It was Peter McGrother, one of your nephews in England that gave us your address. Two months before he died, my father asked me to do

29

something for him, in fact, he put it in his will. He wanted me to bring a lock of his hair back to his family home and bury it there. He set aside enough money for this purpose and because I am his namesake and the only one of his son's not wed, it is only right that I should undertake such a task and honour his dying wish. I shall be arriving in Ireland sometime in mid-October, God willing, and look forward to meeting you and your family.'

Jamie raised his eyes from the letter, "Well now, what do you make of that, Da?"

"We are already well into October, he could arrive any day. I must speak with Mary-Anne about a room for him," James was pulling his trousers on.

It had been quite a while since Jamie had seen his father so alert. Not since before the death of his older brother, Thomas, some months before.

"I'm sure he will send us word of his arrival in advance, maybe a telegram from the ship. There's no need to get yourself all flustered over it, Da."

"That front door of yours could do with a lick of paint," James looked through the window, ignoring his son's advice. "It looks a fine dry day so I'll start straight after my breakfast," he massaged his stomach. "I think I'll have two eggs this morning. Will you put them into the pot for me? And have some yourself, sure you must be starving."

"Not yet, Da. I'm off to bed to snatch a few hours of sleep. Don't be climbing up any ladders now, will you?" Jamie was happy to see his father so lively but worried he might overdo it. "I can give you some help when I wake up."

******

Many of those transported to Van Diemen's Land ended up in Sydney. By the time Francis McGrother arrived there it was considered an unsuitable place for convicts, having too many temptations that might entice them back to a life of crime. Whenever possible, they were sent to farms out in the bush, far from the city, to work out their sentence.

Up until the late 1830's most convicts served their time as indentured labourers on public works for the government or assigned to private individuals. At the time of the young Monaghan man's transportation the Probation System was in operation, which meant that after two years convicts were allowed to earn their own income but within a restricted area. Those with a record of good behaviour could be granted a Ticket of Leave, giving them a limited choice in their own affairs. On completion of their sentence (seven years in many cases) a convict would be given a Certificate of Freedom.

Francis McGrother was sent to the Illawarra region in New South Wales, where the land was so fertile it produced two crops of potatoes a year. It was ironic that the young Irish convict should find himself harvesting a crop that was inadvertently the cause of his transportation. If his people had not been starving due in part to their main source of food, the potato, being decimated by blight, he would not have stolen a cow in the first place.

When his seven year sentence was up, Francis received his Certificate of Freedom and was allowed to go wherever he wished. By then, he had married an Irish woman from county Mayo and they had already started a family together. Francis had no desire to be a potato farmer but had his heart set on a tract of land on which to raise cattle. The lack of a humble spud might have driven the young Irishman to commit a crime but it was the theft of a cow that brought him to Australia. This ultimately changed his fortune, giving him a life he could only have dreamed of in his native land.

CHAPTER SIX

Patrick shook his head in despair at a photograph in the newspaper he held. He was a slow reader at the best of times, but when the report was about a major disaster it took him even longer to get through the article. Such was his nature, tragic events affecting people he had never even met could disturb him deeply. This one was about a hurricane that hit Galveston, Texas the previous month, leaving the city in ruins and many thousands dead.

"It says here, the men piling up the bodies had to be given whiskey to calm their nerves, they were that distressed," Patrick continued aloud.

"Put that away, love. Such bad news will cast a cloud of gloom over us if we dwell on it," Catherine placed two plates of breakfast on the table, "And we need to be cheerful for Lily's sake. I told Maisie at Mass this morning that she would have to cook her own dinner as we would be spending the rest of the day with her aunt."

Taking a seat opposite her husband, Catherine sighed and shook her head, "Poor Lily, Sunday is when she misses Thomas the most."

As he folded the newspaper, Patrick sighed and agreed with his wife about keeping in good humour.

"It is times like this I almost regret learning to read. Bad news jumps out at you wherever you go, on every billboard in the street and on the front page of all the newspapers. As if it isn't bad enough to see poor, sickly, begging children sitting on every corner you turn."

Catherine sensed another speech in the making and quickly changed the subject. If she let her husband continue in such an unsettling train of thought, he would mull over it for the day and allow it to rob him of his sleep that night.

"Maisie and Sean will be happy to have the place to themselves, you should have seen her eyes light up when I told her we wouldn't be here all day," Catherine was determined to change the mood of their conversation.

"You'd think they'd be used to our company by now, wouldn't you?"

"Ah, Patrick, surely you remember what it was like living with Aunt Rose and Uncle Owen when we first wed. You chased me round the house like a madman whenever we had the place to ourselves."

"Which wasn't often enough," laughed Patrick. "But it's *you* who does the chasing now, isn't it, my love?"

"Ah, go on with you and your foolish talk," Catherine laughed. "Eat your breakfast before it goes stone cold. With Ellen and Jeremiah away for the weekend, Lily has spent her first night alone in God knows how long. I cannot fathom why she refused to have me stay with her last night."

"Because she knows Thomas would want her to become accustomed to life without him, if not for her own sake, for their son's," Patrick smiled sadly at his wife. "I would wish for the same should you ever find yourself in Lily's position."

The conversation was beginning to turn sombre again so Catherine stood up from the table, "Well, let's hope *that* is something I won't have to face for a very long time, God willing."

Patrick saw her eyes rest on the mantle clock and raised both hands in the air before she could remind him once again of their plans for the day.

"I know, I know. You go fix your Sunday bonnet on your charming head, while I fetch my cap and jacket."

Wrestling himself into his good jacket, Patrick was reminded of the bit of weight he had put on over the past couple of years and felt his age come upon him. While he waited for Catherine to fix her hair around the bonnet she placed on her head, flashes of his early years as a young father came back to him. Every time he looked into the mirror to shave he could see he was old enough to be a grandfather but in his head he was still a much younger man, full of spirit and righteous indignation.

No matter what age their children are, many parents will always have a sense of responsibility toward their offspring, and it was no different for Patrick and Catherine. Their eldest, Tom, was well settled in his marriage to his employer's daughter. Lottie was a wonderful, loving wife and mother and had quickly become like a daughter to them both. But Catherine still worried at the least sign of a sniffle from any of them, and at every visit Patrick would enquire about the state of their finances and remind his son that he had some savings put aside, if he was ever in need of any assistance.

It didn't irritate Tom in the least to hear the same thing from his father every week. In fact, it only served as a reminder of how much he was still loved. Tom was very comfortable financially, having become a partner in his father-in-law's newspaper and photography business. As his parents grew older, it was more likely that they would be the ones needing help but Tom knew they would be too proud to ask. This being the case, he had been putting some money into a savings account each month, on their behalf.

Patrick and Catherine's other children, Maisie and Ellen, had also made good lives for themselves at young ages. Their main concern was that Maisie should have a safe delivery of her first baby but apart from that, they knew their girls were happy and healthy.

Whenever Catherine enquired of Ellen as to whether she had met any nice men of late, the reply was always the same – their youngest had no intention of wasting her time on a man when she was so busy with her career. The only worry Patrick had about Ellen was that she would exhaust herself between teaching and studying for even more exams. If she were never to marry, it wouldn't bother him in the least, as long as she was happy with her life. It pleased him that she was great company for Lily, now Thomas was no longer with them.

"Do you think we could buy a nice cake from the new German shop that has just opened near Lily's?"

Patrick looked up from his chair to see Catherine standing by the window, her hat perched on a loosely gathered bun of silver streaked hair.

As he went to open the door he caught the familiar scent of her perfume, one she had worn for many years, and remarked on how pretty she looked.

"I think you should start wearing your reading glasses more often, Patrick. I'm an old woman now," Catherine chided.

"But as bonnie as ever, my love. As bonnie as ever."

CHAPTER SEVEN

A game of cards at Paddy Mac's was always a good cover for their meetings but Sergeant Broderick made sure nobody went home any lighter of pocket at the end of the evening. Everyone got back exactly what they had put into the pot, regardless of who won or lost.

"It isn't fair, you taking all my winnings from me, Sergeant. What do the rest of ye say?" Fergus scowled at the other players.

"That's how we always end the night," Jamie replied. "Why should it be any different this evening?"

Infuriated at not getting the alliance he expected from his brother-in-law, Fergus thrust his chair back and stood to watch Sergeant Broderick count out his money, leaving it in a neatly stacked pile in front of him. Without answering Jamie's question, he snatched the coins from the table before storming off in a temper.

Two of the remaining men quickly pocketed their share of the pot and followed Fergus out of the snug, assuring the sergeant they would catch up with him and calm him down.

"That brother-in-law of yours is in a sour mood of late, Jamie," Sergeant Broderick pushed the younger man's coins towards him.

"That's because he won almost every game this evening. You don't hear him complaining about equal shares when he loses, do you?"

The sergeant laughed, "No, he's happy enough to divide the pot evenly on those nights. Can you stay a bit longer, Jamie? There's something I must tell you, but you cannot breathe a word of it to anyone, especially not the other men."

"Sounds very sinister. I'm not sure I want to hear what you have to say, Sergeant."

Jamie did not like being told secrets, not because he found them difficult to keep, but he feared someone else may reveal them and the finger of blame pointed at him.

"I'm telling you this because I need your help and I know I can trust you, above any of the other men," the sergeant lowered his voice, "There is an informer among us."

"Who?" Jamie was shocked.

The older man shook his head, "I don't know. In fact, I couldn't even hazard a guess as to who it might be. But it's true, Jamie. There can only be so many coincidences before it becomes clear that something else is going on. Do you understand what I'm alluding to?"

"Do you mean the failure of some of our missions of late? Sure, the police and militia are always on the alert for any activity on our part."

"Well it's come to the attention of higher up, Jamie, and I've been told to find out if it's true. If you suspect someone, now is the time to say – before any of us end up paying with our liberty, or our lives, over it."

Jamie took a few seconds before answering, even though his instinct was to immediately defend his comrades.

"How do you know I can be trusted, Sergeant? What if I'm the informer?"

"I don't know anything for sure, Jamie, except that you are least likely to do such a thing. But if it *is* you, I shall soon find out."

"Well, it's not me. And I refuse to believe it's any of the men either. Now, if you'll excuse me, Sergeant, I've a night's fishing ahead of me, so I'll be off."

"I'm sorry to have caused offense, Jamie, but I am only following orders – and I expect you to do the same."

"You have my word. I'll keep an eye out for anything suspicious, much as it galls me to do so," Jamie was thankful the weather had held and a few hours of fishing lay ahead of him. "I'll have plenty of time to think on what you've told me when I'm out in my boat tonight."

Left alone in the snug, Sergeant Broderick sighed deeply before knocking three times on the wooden partition separating the tiny room from the rest of the pub. Johnny Mac appeared with two glass tumblers and a bottle of locally distilled whiskey.

"Have a drink before you go. You look like you could do with it," said Johnny.

"I should never have been asked to do that, not when family is involved."

"Someone had to do it. McGrother is a good man, he won't let us down," Johnny finished his drink in one gulp. "I'm sorry, Sergeant, but I must be sending you on your way. I'm still annoyed about that last fine I had to pay in petty sessions, for serving drink after hours."

As Sergeant Broderick made his way home his brain sifted through every scrap of information he had gathered over the past few months. No one escaped the mental scrutiny, not even his wife, Mary-Anne, nor her adopted son, George. By the time he arrived at his front door his head was pounding. He berated himself for suspecting his own family of passing on information they couldn't possibly have any knowledge of.

The house was in darkness but Mary-Anne had left a cold supper between two plates for him on the kitchen table. She was well used to his nocturnal activities and even if he could have shared his secrets with her, he knew she would refuse to listen. The sergeant's wife had made it clear there was to be no mention of *the cause* in her home, and it was her house, no doubt about it. Hadn't she bought and paid for it with her own money? It would be George's house after her and that was only as it should be.

With these thoughts in mind the sergeant climbed the stairs, his stomach satisfied but his head still agitated. As soon as he was snugly nestled in the warm bed beside his wife a thought hit him like a bolt of lightning. He tried to dismiss it by silently arguing with himself over how ludicrous it was, but it wouldn't go away and snapped at him like an annoying terrier.

After a night of fitful sleep, Sergeant Broderick woke up to the loud rattle of a cup and saucer landing on the small wooden locker that stood by his bed.

"You've chores to do in the garden, Sergeant. George had to leave earlier than usual for work this morning."

At the mention of Mary-Anne's son the imaginary terrier was back and this time it bit hard into Sergeant Broderick's conscience and wouldn't let go. He winced with the anguish of it and his wife noticed.

"Is your head pounding from the drink last night? Or is it the thought of having to do some labouring that has you looking like a train ran over your foot?"

"Would you not have a bit of sympathy for an old man? You've a tongue on you that would slice a rock in two this morning. What has you so hot and bothered, greeting me with a sour face instead of a sweet smile?" the sergeant was inwardly beating back the invisible dog.

"When did I ever greet you with a sweet smile in the morning?"

"I was hoping you might start today, love."

Mary-Anne stopped bustling around the bedroom and took a long hard look at her husband. He seemed to be genuinely in great discomfort and her voice softened.

"Your tea is sweet enough without me adding to it," she opened the window and looked towards the henhouse at the bottom of the garden. "I'll fetch the eggs, you stay in bed a wee bit longer. The chores can wait."

Before leaving the room, Mary-Anne planted a kiss on the bald spot on the top of his head and was downstairs before the sergeant had a chance to recover. Such a rare show of affection should have lifted his spirit but it had the opposite effect. How was he to think rationally about informers when one of the suspects might be his own step-son? It was bad enough when he had to make sure it was not Jamie McGrother passing on the information, but to have to clear George's name would be even more upsetting.

Sergeant Broderick drained his china cup before placing it back on the saucer. When the sound of hens clucking reached his ears he was tempted to get dressed and tackle the garden. The work might distract him for a while from the assignment he knew he must fulfil, regardless of his feelings about it. But he was too weary even to dress himself and decided to lay back down, resting his head on one of the new feather pillows Mary-Anne had recently bought for them.

As soon as he closed his eyes the thought of George passing on information crowded out everything else, including the sound of the clucking hens, now directly under his bedroom window. His mind held onto it like a dog with a bone and Sergeant Broderick finally admitted to himself that if *he* could suspect the young man then others might, too.

Although his mother never allowed her son to show even the slightest interest in his stepfather's clandestine activities, George would have been well aware of the sergeant's affiliation to the Irish Republican Brotherhood. Over the years, there had been the usual clashes between father and son, and George could be a determined young man once he set his mind on something. However, no matter what the circumstances may be, Sergeant Broderick was sure that informing on anyone, let alone family members, was something his stepson would never even think of doing.

This thought lessened the mental anguish the sergeant was going through until another one popped into his head. Could George be in serious trouble and need the reward money? It would be very easy for him to pass on information, after all, one of his closest friends was the son of a local policeman.

CHAPTER EIGHT

Annie and Jamie sat at each side of their stove on a night so bad they wouldn't even put a dog out in it, if they had one. Usually, the inclement weather annoyed the young fisherman, as it prevented him from doing what he loved most – being out in the bay with his crew. Of late, that activity had been soured by an intrusion of negative thoughts, as he attempted to carry out Sergeant Broderick's orders.

The warmth now causing his shoulders to relax had more to do with the pleasure of being in his wife's company than to the blazing coals radiating through the bars of the stove. Jamie's habit of opening the fire door to watch the flames dance and throw shadows across the room usually resulted in a debate with Annie about wasting fuel.

Tonight was an exception, possibly due to the howling wind outside, and Annie seemed as relaxed as her husband in the warm glow. A pile of mending lay in a wicker basket by her feet and she squinted in the lamplight while trying to thread a needle.

"I'll raise the flame a wee bit for you, will I love? You'll hurt your eyes if you carry on in this light," Jamie stood to adjust the height of the wick in a lamp hanging from a hook over the fireplace. His wife rubbed her eyes as she listened to the wind howl at their windows.

"I'm mighty thankful we no longer have that leaking, old thatch over our heads, especially on a night like this," said Annie.

Jamie laughed, "That's not what you said when I brought home the slates, if memory serves me."

"You mean when you *stole* those slates," she admonished but smiled in spite of it.

"Well now, it's not exactly stealing when a ship runs aground on a sandbank and the local fishermen go out of their way to help lighten its load."

It was Annie's turn to laugh, "Ah, go on with you," she stuck the needle in a pin cushion then stretched her feet towards the heat of the stove. "It's been a long day. Bad weather always makes it feel much longer than it is, doesn't it? I'm off to my bed, Jamie."

"I won't be long behind you, love. I might have another sup of tea before I join you."

"Is there something up with Sergeant Broderick?"

Annie's question jolted him from his contentment and he felt like a fish being reeled out of a calm body of water.

"I don't think so. What makes you say that?" Jamie was trying to sound matter of fact.

"He's been quieter than usual of late. Yesterday, while I was answering a question he put to me, a faraway look came into his eyes. It was as if his mind had gone off somewhere else while I was talking," Annie shook her head. "If I didn't know the sergeant as well as I do, I would have been offended."

"Ah, you know what he's like. Mary-Anne has probably been nagging him more than usual," Jamie stood, stretching his arms wide to release the sudden tension from his shoulders. "I'll help

46

you warm up the bed, love. The longing for tea has left me."

He placed himself in front of his wife and took hold of both her hands, giving her his usual expectant grin – one she would have no trouble interpreting.

"I can see from that look on your face you've a different longing on you now," Annie smiled, "But mind you keep your cold feet to yourself."

"I won't take my boots off so," Jamie teased as she led him upstairs to their bedroom.

Next morning, Jamie woke to the noise of his family in the parlour below. Annie was berating their eldest daughter over something he couldn't quite make out, from the muffled voice coming up through the floorboards. But he recognized an angry tone, one that was not often heard in their house. Jamie wondered if his father was down there with them, or still in the bedroom keeping well out of the way.

Just as he was about to roll over and try for a second sleep, his daughter let out a high pitched wail and he sat bolt upright, straining to hear what Annie was saying. There would be no rest for him now, after a cry like that from one of his girls.

When Jamie reached the bottom of the stairs his eldest daughter Mary-Ellen, named after both of her grandmothers, had the red marks of a slap across her cheek. She ran so forcefully into his arms, he almost fell over.

"What have you done to get your ma in such a rage child?"

Annie glared a warning at her husband. He had a habit of interfering with any punishments she meted out to their children and it often resulted in the couple still discussing the 'crime' long after the perpetrator had forgotten it. This time, Jamie sensed the offence must be a serious one indeed, for neither of them had ever slapped their children on the face – a paddled rump was usually discipline enough. Even at that, it was almost always their mother who dealt it out.

"Where's the rest of the children, Annie?" Jamie looked at the closed door to the rear bedroom.

"I've sent them off to school with your da. He has taken wee PJ with him. You will not believe what Mary-Ellen has done. I can hardly believe it myself," she held out her hand towards him.

A coin lay upon her palm and Jamie's first thought was that their daughter had stood on a chair and reached up to the little tin box that held the housekeeping money.

"If you needed to buy something you should have asked us, love. You know better than to steal from your own parents," Jamie made sure his tone was harsh enough to convey his disapproval.

"Oh no, your daughter did not take this penny from the housekeeping. Did you, Mary-Ellen?" Annie was beginning to calm down. "Tell your da where it came from. Go on, girl, tell him."

"From Mr. Desmond," came a shaky reply.

Jamie was puzzled, his daughter had often run errands for their elderly neighbour, when he lived next door with his son, Joseph. Every few weeks she had received a penny for her trouble from the old man.

"And what is wrong with that?" he asked, looking at Annie.

"Old Mr. Desmond did not give this coin to Mary-Ellen. She took it from him – after he died," Annie slapped the penny down onto the table with such force, Jamie felt his daughter jump.

He sat her down on a chair and pulled another for himself in front of it. It was one thing to steal from your parents but quite another to rob an elderly neighbour's house, and a departed one at that.

"Is this true?" Jamie lowered himself onto the chair and looked his daughter in the eye. "Did you steal money from Mr. Desmond's house?"

His heart sank when she nodded, her face the picture of guilt.

"Well, you'll have to put it back wherever you found it. I'll come with you while you tell Joseph how sorry you are and that you'll never do such a thing again," Jamie glanced at his wife, "After that, we'll decide on a fitting punishment for what you've done."

"I can't do that," Mary-Ellen replied, her voice trembling.

"And why not?" demanded her mother.

"Because he's buried now, so I can't put it back."

Both parents looked at their daughter in surprise but it was Jamie who spoke first.

"You're not telling us you took it from his pocket. You picked an old man's pocket? I cannot believe any child of mine would do such a thing."

"No Da. I didn't take the coin out of his pocket, I would never do such a thing," Mary-

49

Ellen gave her mother a sideward glance. "I took it from his eye, at his wake."

Annie buried her face in her hands and wept but Jamie had an almost irresistible urge to laugh. He had done the same thing as a child and knew that it was one of his Aunt Maggie's favourite stories to relate to his children.

"Bless us and save us," cried Annie, "We'll have to bring her up to one of the priests."

Mary-Ellen began to sob loudly again and Jamie wasn't sure which of them needed comforting the most.

"What made you do such a thing, love?" he asked in a hushed tone.

The calmness of her father took the fear away from the young girl and words began to pour out of her.

"Mr. Desmond never got to pay me for last month's errands before he died, but Ma said I shouldn't trouble his son about it. At the wake, myself and Lizzy McArdle were sent in to the bedroom to say a prayer over him before we could have a sandwich. We were stood each side of his bed and I told Lizzy the story Aunt Maggie used to tell us," Mary-Ellen took a deep breath and looked nervously at her mother, then lowered her voice, "The one about you taking the coins from your neighbour's eyes when she was laid out, Da."

"And did she tell you the thrashing I got for that heinous act?" asked Jamie.

"She did. She said you couldn't sit down for a week. But Lizzy said we should take the pennies because Mr. Desmond didn't need them where he was going, and before I could stop her, she had one of them in her fist. Everyone was in the

50

parlour, too busy eating and drinking and talking to notice, but I couldn't stop looking at him. It didn't seem right, him lying there with only one eye covered, so I grabbed the other penny and stuck it in my pocket. If I hadn't, Lizzy would have taken it and she wasn't owed any money at all."

Annie had calmed down at this stage and announced that she was in desperate need of a cup of strong tea. Jamie was struggling to contain a laugh threatening to erupt at any moment.

"Besides," piped up Mary-Ellen when she sensed her parents' change of mood, "It was money that was owed to me. I'm sure I heard Mr. Desmond's voice telling me to take it. So that wasn't really stealing, was it?"

That was enough to send Jamie out of the house and across the road. He leapt over a wall on the beach, built to protect the houses on the main street from the lash of stormy seas, and landed beside James, who was keeping an eye on his grandson PJ. The little boy was too young to attend school with his siblings and was so engrossed in building a sandcastle, he barely noticed his father's sudden appearance.

Jamie took a peek over the wall to make sure he had not been followed, and cried with laughter. Once he started it was impossible to stop and try as he might, he could not get rid of the image of their old deceased neighbour lying with a penny on one eye and his daughter swiping it.

"I take it that wife of yours hasn't killed anyone yet," said James.

His son shook his head, "Did you hear why she was in such a rage, Da?"

"I did not. When I arrived back from taking the children to school I could hear the roars of her before I even got to the door. I thought it best to hide out here for wee while, until she calmed down a bit. Do you think it's safe enough to venture inside now? I'm gasping for a cup of tea."

Jamie related the story of his daughter's debt collecting antics and both men had a good laugh over it.

"You would be a bit of a hypocrite to scold her over that now, wouldn't you, son? I seem to remember you doing much the same thing at her age. In fact, your Aunt Maggie loved to tell the children that story, didn't she?"

Jamie agreed and pointed up to the sky, "Old Mr. Desmond must be laughing as hard as ourselves up there over it. He had a wicked sense of humour, didn't he?"

"He did indeed, and he always paid his debts. It wouldn't do to leave this world owing money to a neighbour's child, now, would it?" James patted his son's shoulder. "Be a good lad and help your old da up off this damp sand. If I don't get that tea soon, I'll die of the thirst and it will be me getting the pennies robbed from my eyes."

Jamie never liked to hear his father joke about his passing and reprimanded him for saying such a thing, as they walked to one of the nearby stone steps that led to a gap in the wall. He plucked his young son, Patrick James, named after both his grandfathers, up from the sand and threw him over his shoulder, turning

52

the boy's protests into laughter by tickling the soles of his bare feet.

"If you grow up as mischievous as your big sister, that's what I'll do to you, PJ, tickle the feet off you," Jamie assured. "No matter how big you get, I'll still be able to throw you over my shoulder. Isn't that right, Granda James?"

The older man laughed and gave the wriggling boy a tickle, "Aye, it is indeed. Sure isn't that why your father behaves himself, for fear of me doing the same thing to him."

As James crossed the main street he thought about his sister Maggie and how she was still influencing the family, long after she had left them. Just before they entered the house, he nudged his son and pointed up to the heavens.

"If old man Desmond is looking down on us, amused at all the fuss, we can be sure Maggie is standing beside him laughing her head off."

CHAPTER NINE

For almost a week, the weather had been ideal for taking the boats out and the fishermen of Blackrock were making the most of it while it lasted. After another good nights fishing Jamie arrived home to find the front door to his cottage wide open. Annie and the children would normally have been asleep for at least another couple of hours, as it was Saturday and school was closed.

Assuming his wife had risen earlier than usual or that his father was up and about, Jamie called out that he was starving and hoped the tea was brewing. As he crossed the threshold of the door, the smell of freshly baked scones made his mouth water but the smile left his face when a strange young man, seated at the table, turned around to greet him.

"That's my son, Jamie. And this is Frank McGrother, youngest son of my cousin Francis," James introduced the men to each other.

"Well, I'm pleased you got here safe and sound, after such a long time at sea," Jamie held out a hand in greeting but took it back almost immediately. "Maybe you should wait till I've scrubbed up before we shake, Francis."

"I'm well used to working hands," their visitor stood up and grabbed hold of the young fisherman's hand, shaking it vigorously. "It's a pleasure to meet you, Jamie, your family have made me feel very welcome. Very welcome indeed."

"Sure why wouldn't they? You being a relative and all. I won't be long," Jamie replied before going into the scullery to wash in a basin of warm water, placed there by Annie.

His Sunday shirt and trousers hung on the indoor washing line and Jamie smiled at his wife's desire to impress their relative. Normally, he would have breakfasted in the clothes he'd spent the night fishing in, unless they were soaking wet. Having washed and changed out of his working clothes, Jamie came back into the kitchen and joined his father and their guest at the table. The genial young visitor seemed to be at ease in their company as he answered questions about his people back in Australia.

"Tell Jamie how much land your family owns," said Annie. "They have a very large dairy herd. And sheep, too. Isn't that so, Frank?"

"It is indeed. But good manners prevents me from bragging about it," their visitor replied.

Frank McGrother had grown up listening to his father's accounts of the life of a tenant labourer in Ireland. He knew how the meagre piece of land in Monaghan, leased by his grandfather, was divided up between each of his five sons until the tiny patches of green could barely support a couple, never mind a family. Those memories made the young man feel uncomfortable mentioning the vast tracts of land he and his brothers had inherited on the death of their father.

"It's not bragging when you are only answering the questions we put to you, son," James pushed a plate of scones across the table. "Have another one, Frank. My daughter-in-law is the best cook in the parish."

"Now who's bragging?" chided Annie.

"Did Annie tell you her own father is a farmer?" asked Jamie. "He took on more land just six months ago. I reckon he's got near enough to twenty acres now. Am I right?" the young man looked at his wife.

"Twenty-two," corrected Annie in a hushed voice.

Jamie was puzzled by the almost apologetic tone his wife used. Normally, the expansion of a relative's farm would have been spoken of with pride, given the history of land ownership in Ireland, or more correctly, the lack of it.

"Young Frank here, and his brothers, have inherited *five thousand* acres between them from their father," said James. "My cousin Francis did well for himself. You should be proud of his achievements, son, and don't fret over someone mistaking your pride as bragging. Anyone who does so is envious of your good fortune."

"My father didn't consider it 'good fortune' to be transported to Australia. He never really spoke of those early years, yet many of his friends – including the father of the Mayor of our town – were convicts, like himself."

"Francis McGrother was always remembered with deep respect in our family. Indeed, that cow he stole fed the whole village at a time when we were so hungry we were cooking rats and telling our children it was rabbit meat," James's face clouded over at the memory. "And he wasn't alone when he took the cow, either, but the others all had families to provide for and Francis was a young bachelor. He couldn't see the sense in all of them risking transportation – or worse. So he made them

56

promise not to breathe a word of their part in the deed to anyone."

James looked up to see three frowning faces around the table, "Ah, enough with all this melancholy talk. Have you been for a walk around the village yet?"

Frank shook his head.

"Well then, it's a fine morning for it. Will you join us, Jamie?"

"No, Da. I've a bit of sleep to catch up on, but I'll meet you later at Paddy Mac's," Jamie smiled at their visitor, "I daresay you'll both work up a fine thirst with all that walking."

It took James and his young cousin quite a while to walk the length of the main street due to the many interruptions by neighbours. Once the introductions were made there was no end to the questions about the young man's homeland. A visitor from America was not an unusual occurrence but relatives arriving in Blackrock from Australia caused quite a stir. Even the description of the long journey over was of interest to the listener.

"Did you take note of how nearly everyone begins the conversation with the weather?" asked James.

"We do the same," Frank replied. "The difference is that we complain about the lack of rain, not the abundance of it."

The young Australian went on to relate how continuous years of drought back home had depleted their livestock to only half of what it normally should be.

"That is why I was able to take the time to come here. My brothers can manage what's left of the stock between them. I think we shall have to look at some other means of earning a wage soon, if these droughts continue for much longer.

"I'm sorry to hear that, son," James commiserated. "It's an awful pity we cannot send some of our Irish weather back with you."

As the men rounded a bend in the road they saw three people standing in the distance. Two of them were young men with bicycles, so deep in conversation with a policeman they didn't notice James and his visitor appear.

"I think we should stop now and start walking back towards the other end of the village – that's where we'll find Paddy Mac's," James turned around.

Frank followed him, surprised at the sudden change of direction. He wondered if the sight of a policeman had anything to do with it and was debating on whether or not he should satisfy his curiosity by asking, when his companion finally spoke.

"Did you recognize one of those young men with the bicycles?" asked James.

"It was George, wasn't it? I met him last night when I arrived at Mary-Anne's house."

"It was. That's one of his friends he was with and the policeman is his father. I didn't want to embarrass young George by walking past them. It would have been a wee bit awkward."

"Why is that? Or should I not ask such a question?"

"It's best you know, Frank. Sergeant Broderick is not too happy about young George's choice of friends but his mother has always encouraged the lad to mix with . . . how should I put this now?"

"I think I know what you're saying. Where I come from, you couldn't throw a stone into a crowd and not hit the son or grandson of a convict. In fact, there are two policemen I know whose grandparents were transported themselves."

"Is that so?" James was impressed, "And do the gentry mix with the offspring of convicts?"

Frank thought for a moment before answering, "There are some who do, but it's often the amount of land you own that earns you their respect. My father always said the more acreage you had, the higher a man lifted his hat in greeting you. I'm inclined to agree with him on that."

"If that were the case here, most of us would barely get a tip to the brim," said James. "Although, things have improved a great deal since your father lived here, rest his soul. With the passing of the Land Purchase Act not so long ago, Irish tenant farmers can now buy out their freeholds with a loan from the government. That's what Annie's father has done."

The Wyndham Land Purchase Act of 1903 set the conditions for the breaking up of large estates, giving tenants the opportunity to own the land they rented. It more or less ended the era of absentee landlordism in Ireland.

"Have you never wanted to own any land yourself, James?"

By the time this question was asked, the two men had arrived at one of the smaller beaches on the north end of the village. Along with the salt baths, they were part of the local amenities that attracted day-trippers and holiday makers alike to Blackrock, offering seclusion for the more demure bathers.

The old fisherman raised an arm and pointed towards the horizon, "Why would I want to borrow money to own a few acres of land? Look at the size of the place where I harvest my food, and I don't have to pay anybody rent to do so. Nor do I have to stay within a boundary, I can bring my boat wherever I choose. My son, Jamie, feels the same way about it."

Frank could see the passion in the eyes of his companion and was reminded of the look that came over his father whenever he gazed across his pastures. As he stood on the rocks, taking in the vastness of the body of water in front of him, he understood why James had no need to seek ownership of the land. But that was an exception to the rule. In early sixteenth century Ireland, Catholics, both Irish and Anglo-Norman, owned all of the land between them.

However, after three hundred years of colonialism, plantations and evictions, about ninety percent of the country belonged to Anglo-Irish Protestant landlords, many of them absentee, and Catholics were forced to become tenants of their own land. To pay their rent, they had to sell their agricultural produce and livestock, or face eviction. Potatoes were nutritious, cheap to buy and grew quite easily in poor soil, without taking up too much space. This is how the vast majority of the Irish population came to be almost completely dependent on one crop.

CHAPTER TEN

"Sean and his brothers have bought a piece of land and they plan on building ten houses, one for each family and six to sell," Maisie beamed as she told her mother the good news.

"Oh love, that's the best news I've heard in a long time," Catherine replied.

"And our Tom wants to buy one of the houses so we can live near each other. Poor Lottie has been longing for her own home ever since their first son was born."

"Well now that her sister has come back from college her father won't be living on his own if they move away, will he?" said Catherine.

"From what Tom tells me, I think old Mr. McIntyre will be happy to have a quiet house again, once they've gone. He can be a bit short with the boys, especially when they are chasing each other around the furniture, their whooping and hollering echoing through that big old house."

"Ah well, that's what happens when you have two boys so close in age, Maisie. Sure they'll be great company for each other when they move out of the city."

The two women carried on sewing as they spoke. Maisie had given up her job in a clothing factory when she married Sean and was now delighted to be expecting their first child. She caressed her seven month bump and sighed.

"If only this wee one could have waited until we had our own roof over our heads."

Catherine understood her daughter's impatience to move into her own home and patted Maisie's swollen belly.

"Well, you cannot do anything about that now, love. Mark my words, you'll be glad to have that baby in your arms instead of your belly, no matter whose roof you are under. It shall not be long before you feel as if you have an elephant in there."

"I already feel like I'm carrying an elephant around with me. Don't tell me it will get worse, Ma," gasped Maisie.

"The last two months are very tiring and babies begin to feel twice as heavy. You must put your feet up every chance you get – else your legs will swell up like pumpkins."

Maisie stuck both feet out and frowned, "They have already. I used to be very proud of my slender ankles. Now look at them."

"Don't worry, it won't be too long before you're back to your old self," assured her mother.

Catherine began to pack their sewing away and remarked on the beautiful day, suggesting a visit to her sister-in-law, Lily.

"The bit of fresh air will do you a power of good, Maisie. We can take a tramcar if you don't feel up to the walk."

Once outside in the air, Maisie began to feel a bit more energetic. She hadn't gone very far, though, when she accepted her mother's offer of a tram ride. The couple filling the seat in front of them looked to be in a bad mood and every few minutes the man would turn to the woman and berate her over some aspect of her appearance or housekeeping skills. The poor woman visibly shrank with each derogatory remark, which created an awkward atmosphere around those who could hear what was said. Maisie and Catherine breathed a sigh of relief, as did the other passengers, when the ill-tempered man disembarked, followed by his unfortunate, downtrodden companion.

"Would you say they were married, Ma?"

"I reckon so, otherwise I don't see why that poor woman would put up with such disgraceful treatment."

"Aren't we blessed to have two fine men who treat us like queens?" Maisie sighed contentedly.

"I have to admit, your Sean spoils the life out of you, no doubt about it," said Catherine. "You picked a good man in him."

"Da is a good husband, too, isn't he? And a great father to us. I shall be happy if Sean is even half as good to this wee one. He says when he gets our house built we're going to fill it with children. I think I'd like six, Ma. Three boys and three girls. That's enough, don't you think?"

"Aye, Maisie. Six is plenty." Catherine looked around the half-empty carriage, then lowered her voice. "Do you remember what I told you about spacing out your babies?"

"Yes Ma, please don't go over that again," Maisie checked the seat behind them and was relieved to find it unoccupied. "I was a bit shocked that you would want me to do such things. When I asked Sean if he knew about these matters he laughed so hard, I went as red as a tomato. He said he was surprised that a good Catholic woman like yourself would encourage her daughter in such heathen practises and that his own mother would never approve of interfering with God's will."

"Seeing as she had eleven children, I doubt she would. I consider myself a good Catholic, Maisie, but the Pope won't be feeding any of my offspring, so I don't see why he should be telling me it's wrong to do my best to keep my family to a size I can afford to look after."

Maisie looked down at her bump and smiled, "Well, jumping up and down a hundred times didn't stop this wee one from being made."

Catherine burst out laughing as a memory from some months back came to mind and her daughter smiled when she shared it with her.

"If only your Sean knew how much your father and myself laughed over that, he would never be able to look us in the eye again."

"You must never tell him, promise me, Ma," Maisie pleaded. "It was bad enough that Da came out of your bedroom while I was jumping up and down like a mad woman in the parlour that night. I knew by the way he apologized for interrupting me that he had a suspicion as to why I was behaving like a lunatic."

"He is well used to seeing me do the same thing. Not that we have to worry about that anymore, thanks be to God. Your father always did his best but just in case he hadn't been quick enough to . . ."

"*Ma*, would you stop," Maisie cried. "You're embarrassing the life out of me now. I don't want to hear anymore."

"Well, after this wee one arrives you must tell Sean you want a nice big gap between babies and start jumping as soon as he's finished . . . you know . . . well as quick as you can afterwards. That is, if you don't want to have children like steps of stairs, Maisie."

The young woman agreed to speak to her husband that very evening if her mother would change the subject and was saved any further embarrassment upon reaching their stop.

Lily was in a surprisingly good mood when her visitors arrived. She had received a letter from her father-in-law, James McGrother, and it had cheered her up no end.

"Did he write to you, too, Catherine?" she asked.

"No, he didn't. That's strange, normally he sends a bundle of letters at the same time. What did he say, or is it personal? I'm sorry, Lily, I shouldn't be so nosey," Catherine apologized.

Lily took an envelope from a drawer in the bureau that had belonged to her late husband. It was where Thomas had written all his reports and articles for the newspaper he had worked for and it remained in the parlour as a comforting reminder of him, much as his bicycle did, still standing where he had left it in the hallway.

"Not at all, sure didn't I have to get your Ellen to read it to me," Lily smiled warmly as she handed it to her sister-in-law. "Would you mind reading it aloud, Catherine? I'd like to hear what it says again."

It was typical of James to think of his young widowed daughter-in-law even though his own heart was breaking. The letter was full of wonderful memories of Thomas's childhood years and some of the stories recounted were new to Catherine herself. After listening to the six neatly scripted pages being read, all three women had tears in their eyes.

"Heavens above, Grandad James knows how to write a good letter, doesn't he, Ma?" Maisie wiped a tear from her cheek.

"He does, love. I suppose that's where our Thomas got his way with words," Catherine gave a quick glance at Lily and was relieved to see a smile on her face.

"I wish I could write back to him in my own hand but I've never been able to get a grasp on reading and writing. Ellen said she would write down what I'd like to say when she returns from her classes this evening."

"Would you not ask Jeremiah to write it instead, Lily? What did he say when he read the letter from Da?"

Lily's face clouded over, "I haven't let him read it. He doesn't know it arrived. I'm not sure how he will take it, Catherine, he rarely mentions his father and I'm reluctant to bring up Thomas's name when in his company."

Maisie felt compelled to speak, even though she knew her words might cause offense. Clearing her throat, the young woman prepared herself for her mother's berating.

"I think Jeremiah is afraid to speak about Uncle Thomas for fear of causing you more pain, Aunt Lily, so he bottles up his feelings. Remember how you locked yourself away in your room for days on end after the funeral and how worried the lad was about you?"

As expected, Catherine jumped to Lily's defence, "Maisie, apologize immediately to your aunt. She had every right to be upset, she had just lost her husband."

Lily hushed her sister-in-law, "There's no need for an apology. Maisie is right, I was so busy drowning in my own grief I completely ignored how Jeremiah must have been feeling. I'm going to give him that letter after supper and he can read it in his own good time."

CHAPTER ELEVEN

From his seat by the window, James scrutinized the passing countryside for any familiar landmarks. The last time he had been on a train was a trip to Dublin to spend a day with his youngest daughter, who lived there, and he savoured the memory of his last visit. Every year, close to the anniversary of her mother's death, Breege invited her father to the house where she lived in Sandymount, just a couple of miles from the city centre. She worked as a cook for a solicitor's family and had an attic room with a view over the sea on Strand Road.

"How long has it been since your last visit?" Frank's voice interrupted James's reminiscing.

"To Dublin?"

"No, to where you grew up, James," the young man frowned as he peered through the window, hoping they had boarded the train heading in the right direction. "This *is* the train to Carrickmacross, isn't it?"

Feeling a bit foolish at being caught daydreaming, James adjusted his cap, "Of course it is, sure we're heading north not south," his eyes swept across the patchwork of fields. "I have not been back to my old parish since the day I left with my family."

Noting the older man's discomfort, Frank thanked him for accompanying him on the journey and tried to change the subject, but James continued speaking about the past.

"There were no trains in those days, we walked the twenty mile journey to Dundalk.

68

That's not too far to go on a full stomach but when you're half-starved and carrying young children it can take its toll on your strength. My poor Mary was with child, so we stayed in Blackrock with my uncle Pat, while the rest of my brothers and sisters went on to England."

"Did you not join them later?" asked Frank.

"Oh, I did for a while. But my heart was always here, in Ireland, so we came back. Blackrock has been home to me since then. When I was four years old my parents died and my brothers would send me to stay with my aunt and uncle in Blackrock every summer, until I was old enough to leave school and work the fields with them. Your father came with me one year but he only lasted a week. He wasn't too fond of the water, as I recall, but I was out on my uncle's boat at every opportunity."

"How old was he then?" asked Frank, having never heard that story before.

"I would say he was about the age of eight. Francis was only two years older than me. I remember him begging to go with me that summer. Normally he would have been working the fields but his father gave in because Francis had never seen the sea," James laughed at the memory. "And after that first trip out on the boat, he never wanted to see it again. He heaved all the way out into the bay and all the way back to shore. Uncle Pat and the other men teased the life out of him, thanking him for their bulging nets, on account of the amount of bait he was supplying. I cannot imagine how much he must have been ailing on that crossing to Australia."

"That's one of the reasons he never came back to Ireland when he got his Certificate of Freedom," said Frank. "I know he suffered from terrible bouts of seasickness, he told us he almost died on the ship."

James couldn't help remarking on how well his cousin's fortune had changed because of his transportation, harsh punishment that it was for him.

"My father used to say being sent to Australia was the best and the worst thing that ever happened to him. Not long before he died, he told me he felt as if he was carrying a great big hole in his heart where part of it had been left behind in Ireland. I would feel the same way should I be forced to leave my homeland."

As he spoke, Frank looked through the window at the rolling hills, with their dense crown of trees, rising up from the lush green landscape. It was quite different from the one that had surrounded him all of his life.

The rest of their journey was spent reminiscing on their own very different childhoods, with James speaking mostly of the sea and Francis describing the vast open tracts of land his father had accumulated over the decades.

Eventually, the train pulled into Essexford, it's small, redbrick stationmaster's home looking more like a level crossing house rather than the two-storied accommodation usually provided by the railway company. After a brief stop, it continued its short journey to the end of the line at Carrickmacross.

Once they had made their way to the town's wide main street, James looked around for somewhere to eat a midday meal. A homely little restaurant caught his eye and he crossed the street to peer through its one large window. James nodded to Francis and assured him the food was bound to be good and affordable, on account of the large number of diners inside.

During the course of their meal, James struck up a conversation with an elderly man at the table next to them. The weather was discussed, as was usual, before inquiries were made as to who James's people were. In spite of his many years away from the area, he still had a local accent, which became more pronounced the longer he listened to it.

James identified which branch of the McGrother family he was from and explained their reason for being in Carrickmacross. He was in turn told of the old man's family who were called Rice.

"Well now, what do you think of your father's country?" Mr. Rice directed his question to Frank.

"From what I've seen, it's just as my father described it. I like how green it is and how near to each other your towns are."

"But Australia will always be your home, am I correct in saying that?" James added.

Frank didn't want to cause offence and paused to give a diplomatic but honest answer. The two older men exchanged smiles at his obvious discomfort.

"It's only natural for you to feel attached to the land you were born and raised in, lad. The pity of it is that too many of our sons and daughters had to leave. But some of them made a good life for themselves, my own children

71

included," Mr. Rice said. "At least their leaving was by choice, not like those unfortunates in the *poor man's jail*."

Frank gave James an inquiring look and was told the man was speaking of the workhouse.

"In fact, thirty-eight young orphan girls were sent out to your part of the world from the poorhouse here in this town," Mr. Rice continued.

"To Australia?" asked Frank.

"Aye, their only crime was poverty and not having a home. Some of them were as young as fourteen," was the reply.

"Are you speaking of the Earl Grey women? But they were not transported as convicts. My mother came out that way and was placed as a domestic with a settler family. That was all she ever told us about her past."

"She must have been in the poorhouse, so, and didn't have much of a choice," replied Mr. Rice.

"She was sixteen and the only one left of her family when she went into the workhouse in Mayo. I think the memories were too painful for her to dwell on, she never spoke of Ireland like my father did."

"My family lost everything in our efforts to stay out of the workhouse," said James. "In the end, to avoid dying from the hunger or the fever, my brothers and sisters took the assisted passage to England. My wife was with child so I stayed in Blackrock with my aunt and uncle. In time, we joined the family in Sunderland and lived there for some years but we missed Ireland too much and came back to Blackrock, where I fished with my uncle."

"Ah, so you're a fisherman, then," said Mr. Rice.

"I am, for my sins," replied James. "My youngest son has his own boat now and it keeps a roof over our heads, thanks be to God."

"Were you here in Carrickmacross when Mitchell died?" asked Mr. Rice.

James laughed and slapped his knee, "Indeed I was. What a night. Did your father ever tell you about that, Frank?"

"Was it the time the bonfires were lit on every hilltop to celebrate his death?" the young Australian replied.

Mr. Rice responded with a hearty laugh, "Ah! That was a wonderful sight to behold. Mitchell's passing was the answer to many a prayer. He was a cruel, cruel man, who raised our rents the minute he took up his appointment as an agent for the landlord. My mother had always taken pride in her home but after that, she refused to let my father whitewash the walls nor paint the door."

"Why was that, sir?" asked Frank.

"Because if your house looked too good, your rent went up, son," said James.

"Aye, and Mitchell was quick to spot any improvement. It was him that put a rent on the bogs that had always been free to cut," Mr. Rice added.

James sighed and nodded his head, "I remember that. Our family had to pay £18 for the three acres we had between us. As if it wasn't enough facing the threat of hunger, Mitchell added the prospect of a cold winter and no way of cooking your food, if you couldn't afford to rent a piece of bog."

73

The two older men sat in silent contemplation, as people are inclined to do when reflecting upon the shared hardship of past times. Frank was about to reach out towards his cup but changed his mind, afraid to disturb an almost sacred moment by the movement. As if he had read the young man's thoughts, Mr. Rice lifted his head and tapped his fingers on the table.

"Well, that's enough reminiscing for today. There is a family bearing your name, here in the town, and I know who to ask about them."

The older man left them and went into the kitchen to pay his regards to the cook, who was one of his nieces. Ten minutes later, he returned bearing good news.

"There are McGrother's living in O'Neill Street. He is a blacksmith. I can walk that way and introduce you to them, my niece went to school with his wife."

The family in O'Neill Street turned out to be distant relatives of James and Frank and after numerous cups of tea and sharing of news spanning more than fifty years, the blacksmith sent his son, Mattie, out to hitch up a pony and trap. It was agreed the boy would bring their two visitors to the place where Frank's father had once lived. The offer of a bed for the night had been made but James replied that he must return to Blackrock on the evening train. Frank would have stayed but sensed his cousin's unease at being in the place of his youth.

The boy told them there wasn't much to see where they were going but James assured Frank no matter what state of ruin they might find it in, he would know which house had once

74

been Francis McGrother's family home. On the way, they passed a track leading to a hill covered by trees and shrubs. It looked very much like the place where James had first kissed his wife and Mary's youthful smile came into his head, bringing on an ache he had been struggling to avoid ever since he stepped off the train.

"Did you want to stop here, James?" Frank's voice cut into his thoughts.

"No, no, son. I was just reminded of something by the landscape. It's a wee bit discomforting, to come to the place of your youth and feel like a stranger."

Every time the name of a neighbour or distant relative came to mind, James asked young Mattie if he knew anything of them, but the answer was always the same – he had never heard of them, but maybe his father could help. James finally resigned himself to the fact that some families had simply disappeared, leaving no trace behind in a land that had once been called home by generations of their ancestors.

They came to a halt at a place that James found difficult to recognize. He looked around and saw what used to be a track, covered over with grass and briars.

"This is where my father said I was to bring you," the boy explained. "It's all overgrown now, but if you follow that track you'll come to the place you've been looking for."

Frank helped his cousin down from the trap and wondered why there wasn't at least a ruined house in sight. He realized the stones might be covered over by foliage and for the first time doubted if he would be able to locate his father's family home.

"How do you know this is the place, maybe we need to go on a bit further, son," James was worried at how unfamiliar everything around him looked.

The boy pointed to a high stone wall in the distance, explaining that it was the boundary of the landlord's estate. He could see James was puzzled and felt sorry for the old man with such a lost look on his face.

"I think the houses you are searching for are in those walls yonder," Mattie said, as he jumped down from the trap and broke a few branches from a hawthorn hedge. "Do you want me to lead the way? We can cut through the brambles with these sticks. Maybe we can find where they once stood."

James didn't move an inch but kept staring at the wall on the other side of a wide expanse of pastureland, sheep scattered across it. Where had the fields of barley and oats gone? For a moment they came back to him and if he squinted his eyes, James could see his cousin, Francis, in the distance, labouring alongside his father. The vision appeared so real to him, he almost raised a hand to catch their attention.

"I'm sorry, Frank. You've come all this way only to find a tangle of brambles and not even a broken wall of your father's house to see."

"What shall I do now, James? I cannot fulfil my father's dying wish here, can I?" Frank looked around in dismay. "I was hoping to bury the lock of hair within the walls of his house."

Young Mattie, moved by the men's disappointment, looked at the landlord's wall, spread out as far as the eye could see, "I reckon most of the empty ruins around these parts were used to build that ugly monster," he spat on the ground in disdain.

James agreed and began to climb up onto the trap, "Come on boys, we had best be on our way. There's nothing here for us – not anymore."

"But do you not want to carry on to where your own house stood?" asked Frank. "Now that we're here, you might as well see if there's anything left of it."

Shaking his head, James gestured for his cousin to take a seat, "I doubt I'll find anything more than what we have here, an old track covered in brambles. Am I right, son?" he addressed the boy.

"I reckon you are, Mr. McGrother. I think it would be a waste of time, if you're looking for a house, that is. Would you not ask one of the priests in town to have a look in the church records? They are always getting letters from America asking about someone or other."

The two men smiled as the same thought entered their heads. If they could find a grave belonging to Frank's grandparents it would be the next best thing to finding their house.

"How do you know they get letters from America?" asked James.

"I was an altar boy up to a year ago and many a Sunday, before Mass, the two priests would be disputing over whose turn it was to answer the letters. By the sound of it, they must have had one every week."

"Well now, get this pony to go as fast as you can, son. We have a call to make at the priests' house. Let's hope one of them is there when we get back to town," James said, smiling at the look of relief on Frank's face.

Because James himself had been born in the county, the parish priest reluctantly dropped what he was doing to look through the burial records. He would have preferred a bit more time, but seeing as they were on his doorstep he asked them to go to the cemetery and search the headstones while he looked through the church records.

Saint Joseph's cemetery was within walking distance of the town, but the blacksmith's son said he would bring them there in the pony and trap and help with their task. He was only too happy to be out in the fresh air and away from the heat of the forge, where he had been working with his father since leaving school.

Between the three of them, it wasn't long before every headstone had been scrutinized but not one McGrother nor McGroder could be found. James knew that due to many of his relatives' inability to read and write, the family name was often recorded with either spelling.

"Maybe the priest will have better luck with the church records than we're having here," said Frank.

"Do you think some of your family ended up in the workhouse?" it was a logical question from Mattie.

Both men stared at whatever gravestone they were standing in front of, and fell silent. The thought had indeed crossed their minds but it was one they had dismissed immediately. The workhouse was not a suitable place to leave

Frank's father resting, even symbolically, in his native homeland.

"I'm sure something has turned up in the records, Frank. Come along now, you two, let's be getting back. There's no use wasting any more time here," James tried his best to sound hopeful and positive.

The priest wasn't having any better luck finding Frank's grandparents in the pages of decades he was scanning. If his predecessors had taken more care with their script it would have made the search a lot easier, but the family name was an easy one to find, once you knew what you were looking for – even if it had been misspelled.

There was one particular set of records that might throw some light on the whereabouts of the resting place of the young Australian's grandparents, but it was the last place anyone would want to find the name of a relative.

When James and Frank arrived back at the parochial house the news was not very good. After apologizing for being unable to find the whereabouts of a family grave for the two men to pray over, the priest suggested they leave it with him and he would contact nearby churches to see what could be found of Frank McGrother's grandparents. To prepare them for the worst, he said he would find out if there was any mention of them in the workhouse records, too. The look on their faces was one the priest had seen whenever someone turned up on his doorstep inquiring about a family member, only to learn they had ended their days in the workhouse. Usually, he relayed this information by letter and it spared him the discomfort he now felt at the humiliation such a possibility brought on.

"There's no shame in being poor, son. We are all equal in God's eyes."

The priest's words were meant to comfort but the mention of being poor made Frank bristle. Sensing the mounting tension, James took hold of his young cousin's arm and led him away, bidding good day to the parish priest.

"Come now, Frank, we had best be saying our goodbyes to that nice family in O'Neill Street. If we don't make our way to the station soon, we'll miss the last train back. The priest has my address, no doubt we'll hear something soon enough."

While they waited for the evening train to Dundalk, Frank was still bothered by the thought that his grandparents might have spent their last days in a workhouse, only to end up buried in an unmarked grave. He decided to remain in Carrickmacross to do some more searching and asked James if he should take the blacksmith up on his offer of a place to stay.

"Of course you should, them being distant relatives and all. Given a wee bit more time, they might remember something that would help in your search."

"Will you be alright traveling alone, James? I can always come back here on tomorrow's train."

"Ach, now you're sounding like my son, fretting over me. Off you go and arrange your lodgings. I shall see you when I see you, there is no need to be hurrying back to Blackrock."

"I'd like to wait until you board the train, at least. I feel close to my father when in your company, James. You remind me of him, not so much in looks but in your manner and your way of speaking."

The older man nodded and the two of them sat together making light conversation as they observed the other passengers arrive in dribs and drabs, until the sound of a whistle caught their attention.

From his seat by the window, James watched the tall, straight figure of Frank McGrother grow smaller as the speed of the train stretched out the distance between them. It was as if he was looking at his cousin Francis, and the days of his youth with all its memories came flooding back, bringing with them a mixture of pleasure and pain. The faces of long gone relatives flashed clearly before his eyes, obscuring his view of the passing fields, and the urge to reach out to them was almost irresistible.

James placed his fingertips against the windowpane when his beloved Mary appeared, her warm smile bringing a lump to his throat. He recalled how wary she was of the stormy sea, the day they first arrived in Blackrock, and at his juvenile attempts to apologize for the weather. It was her first time at the coast and James had revelled in the look of awe on his wife's face the following morning, when she stood on the shore across from Uncle Pat's cottage and dipped her toe into the calm water.

But it was the appearance of his eldest son among those departed loved ones that drew a tear from the old fisherman's eye. James had momentarily forgotten about Thomas's death and grief instantly stabbed at his heart. He gave a quick glance around the half-filled carriage and prepared himself for the surge of emotion threatening to overwhelm him. Pulling the collar of his jacket around his ears and drawing his cap low over his eyes, James sank into his shoulders. With his head resting against the window, he feigned sleep, and gave himself up to the rhythmic movement of the train.

CHAPTER TWELVE

Jeremiah came through the door flushed with excitement. At first, his mother thought he might have been ill and automatically put a hand to his forehead as he kissed her cheek.

"I'm fine, mother. I must tell you what I've been listening to while the words still ring in my ears."

The young man began to relate a speech that had obviously stirred something within him, judging by the animated way he spoke. It was all about freedom for Ireland from oppressive rule and the need to support those on the home soil, who were readying themselves for that great day of independence.

"Stop such talk at once, young man," demanded Lily. "I won't have you listening to the likes of that, do you hear me?"

"But father would have taken notes and reported it in his column. I have Irish blood running through my veins. You have, too, mother, or are you suddenly ashamed of your heritage?"

The reply to his question came in the form of a sharp slap across the face, which hurt more than any thumps or punches received in schoolyard scuffles. It was the first time Lily had ever done such a thing and she regretted it the instant her palm made contact with her son's cheek.

"Look where your father's reporting got him – into an early grave. Do you think I want you to risk having the same fate? Stay away from such gatherings, Jeremiah. I forbid you to even listen from a distance."

Without uttering a word, the young man turned away from his mother and went into his bedroom, slamming the door behind him. As Lily stared at the spot where he had been standing, just seconds before, she allowed the old familiar feeling of despair replace the fear her son's words had brought on.

Seething with indignation in his room, young Jeremiah assumed his mother had struck him in anger. He didn't realize it was fear that caused her to react the way she had, not rage. How could he know that every morning, when he left home for college, Lily struggled to keep perceived dangers of what could befall him from her mind? Some days, she imagined him struck by a tram or trampled under the hooves of a horse. At other times, the vision of her son being set upon by thieves and beaten to death, like his father, refused to leave her mind until Jeremiah's safe return.

This new threat was one her imagination had not previously forced upon her. Now she had the fear of her son being caught up in a riot to add to her list of possible dangers. Lily decided to enlist the help of her sister-in-law and her husband in dealing with this latest worry. She was sure they would see her fear as genuine and not dismiss it as the paranoia of an overprotective parent.

Through his locked bedroom door, Jeremiah adamantly refused to accompany his mother to the Gallagher home, citing a headache as an excuse. He guessed the reason for the visit and had no intention of receiving another well-meaning lecture from his Uncle Patrick.

By the time Lily arrived at her relatives' door she had worked herself up into a right state. Catherine knew by the look of her that she was distraught and led her to one of two comfortable armchairs set each side of a small circular table. A vase of flowers on its centre caught the sunlight from the nearby window that looked out onto the street below.

"Is this new, Catherine? It has a lovely grain," as Lily ran her fingers across the smooth, polished oak, she noticed the sewing machine was missing from the room. "You haven't given up sewing have you?"

"That table was a present from our Tom for our last wedding anniversary but I kept it in the bedroom because there was no room for it in here. Only the other day, Patrick said we should put it there, by the window. He said it was far too good to be hidden away."

Catherine set a tray on the table and began to pour some tea, "Now we sit here at the end of the day, getting the last bit of light before dark, and I have to admit he was right."

"But where have you put your machine, Catherine?"

"In my bedroom, Lily. Sure that's where I've always stored my mending, so as not to taint it with the smell of cooking. When Maisie and Sean move out I shall have a spare room to use for my sewing."

"Oh, would you not take in some lodgers and save yourself all that work."

"I did think about it but I like sewing, and besides, lodgers can be hard work. If they're men, I would be expected to do their laundry and provide their meals. If they're women I would most likely have to share my kitchen with them and worry like a mother over the company they were keeping," Catherine frowned. "No, I shall stick to the sewing."

"Speaking of worrying like a mother – I need to ask you something," Lily lifted up the lace curtain and peered through the window.

Catherine waited patiently. She was well used to Lily arriving unexpectedly, ever since her brother, Thomas, had passed away. Widowhood is always difficult to adapt to but for her sister-in-law it had been exceptionally hard, having lost a husband who had provided everything for her, and not just in a material or financial sense. Every minute that he wasn't working or on a cycle ride with his son, Thomas spent with Lily. They went everywhere together and neither had a wide circle of friends, not even as a couple.

"Jeremiah has been listening to political talk. It's gotten him all riled up about Irish freedom and such nonsense. I'm afraid he'll get hurt, Catherine."

"You mean like his father did?"

Lily nodded, hoping her sister-in-law would understand, being a mother herself.

"This country gained its freedom, why shouldn't Ireland do the same?" was the unexpected reply.

"Do you mean to tell me you're a Fenian now?" Lily was shocked.

Shaking her head, Catherine smiled sadly, "No, I'm not. But I understand what moves a person to become one. Sure, look at my Patrick.

He has been a radical at heart since before I ever knew him. The shame of his family having to go into the workhouse and then losing his mother there has stuck with him all through his life, even though he was only a wee child at the time. I dread to think what he might do, should the world's governments declare justice for the poor and a fair wage for all workers. He would have nothing to rant about."

"Maybe he would become a Fenian," Lily suggested.

Both women looked aghast for a moment then broke into laughter. Releasing the morning's tension did Lily a power of good and she felt the weight of anxiety lift from her shoulders.

"Would you like Patrick to have a word with Jeremiah? Or maybe our Tom, he looks up to him and sees him as an older brother, doesn't he?"

Lily was quiet as she thought about Catherine's suggestion. Eventually, she heaved a weary sigh and patted her sister-in-law on the arm.

"I'm feeling less worried already, having shared my burden with you, and I'm grateful you didn't call me a silly woman for allowing such nonsense to get the better of me. I think I shall leave it a while yet, before I bring someone else into this latest problem between myself and my son. But I would be happy for you to share what I've told you with Patrick and get his advice on it."

"Of course I can do that, Lily. My husband can be very discreet about such matters, no doubt he'll find an opportunity to bring this up with Jeremiah without him feeling he is being admonished at the request of his mother."

"Thank you Catherine, where would I be without you? Your family have been a tower of strength to us since Thomas's passing, and your Ellen couldn't be more loving, especially to Jeremiah. It was a blessing indeed, the day she came to live with us."

CHAPTER THIRTEEN

Keeping his disturbing suspicions from Mary-Anne was becoming increasingly difficult for Sergeant Broderick. It was a good job she found it difficult to read him and for that reason had never put much effort into questioning him during his more pensive moments. Not for the first time, he found himself thankful for his wife's disinterest in his subdued preoccupation. She was a very independent woman, in every way, and it was a quality that seemed to grow stronger with the passage of time.

All through George's college years, the sergeant had never once complained about the money spent on his stepson's education. The new uniform, tailor made for him at the start of each school year to accommodate the extra inches he had grown, was never a bone of contention between the couple. Mary-Anne would not see the boy wearing second-hand clothes, under any circumstances. She saved a large part of her money from the summertime business of her lodging house to have her son turn up at college in a well-fitting, brand new uniform that would have anyone who didn't know him think he was of the gentry.

The fact that George was such a quiet lad made it more difficult for his stepfather to make a decision about where the young man's loyalties lay. He had spent much of his childhood and teenage years with his grandfather and James McGrother's personality had definitely rubbed off on the boy.

Sergeant Broderick's thoughts turned to his father-in-law. For James, when it came to alliances, only one stood far above anything else – his family. He kept his nose out of other people's business and seemed to be able to see both sides of an argument. Although he was well above suspicion of being an informer, the sergeant wondered how far James would go in protecting one, should they turn out to be a member of his own family.

"Have your elbows rusted up?" Mary-Anne's voice snapped him out of his mental debating. "You've had your arms stretched out across the table for a good ten minutes. Seeing as our George will be staying in town for the weekend you can do his chores," she placed a cup of steaming tea between his hands. "Did you notice he's been acting strange of late? I hope he hasn't gotten himself a sweetheart, he's still too young for all that nonsense."

"Now you mention it, the lad has been a bit quieter than usual," the sergeant replied. "But if it's a lass that's causing it, then we cannot be too hard on him. It's only natural, after all."

As his wife continued to voice her opinion on their son's suspected romance, Sergeant Broderick leaned back in his chair, half-listening, and tried to convince himself that romance was most likely the reason for George's many overnight stays in Dundalk, of late. He wished with all his heart that it was the case but his head was telling him otherwise.

"Have your ears stopped working along with your arms?" Mary-Anne's voice cut into her husband's thoughts.

"Sorry, love. What was it you said?"

"I said, the place will be packed full of townspeople with this event his lordship is holding. You know what men are like when there's any kind of a race going on," Mary-Anne was referring to the horse racing often held on the beach at Blackrock, and gave a disapproving frown.

"Well they won't be taking any of my money, that's for sure," her husband replied. "You've never known me to be a gambler, have you?"

The sergeant received a kiss on the cheek, which took him by surprise.

"No, there's plenty round here that would bet on two spiders climbing a wall, but you're not one of them, my love, and I'm thankful for that."

As quickly as the smile spread across Sergeant Broderick's face, it disappeared with his wife's next words.

"I know I can rely on you to help me in the kitchen when the tearoom fills up with all those hungry visitors, seeing as our George won't be here to lend a hand."

The sergeant sighed and nodded, he had hoped to spend the day mingling with the crowds, watching the races on the beach. For him, there was nothing more exhilarating than the sight of horses on the gallop, it was one of the few pleasant memories he had from his army days. The thunderous vibration of their hooves pounding the earth never failed to make his heart race and his pulse quicken.

But Sergeant Broderick was not inclined to reminisce for too long about that particular period of his life and quickly suppressed a disturbing image of dead and injured animals, their limbs intertwined with their equally afflicted riders, having bravely charged into battle.

******

A selection of stalls had been set up along the wall that divided the main street from the beach and Annie herded her children past them, only stopping to buy some periwinkles being sold by an elderly neighbour. The village was heaving with locals and visitors, all in good spirits with the fine weather and holiday atmosphere.

Bumping into her husband, Annie was surprised to find him in a heated discussion with two of her brothers. At the sight of their sister, both men stormed off barely saluting her.

"What was all that about, and why aren't you in your boat taking visitors around the bay?"

"I should be, Annie," replied Jamie. "But your brother Fergus came begging for my takings to pay a gambling debt. When I refused he caused a ruckus and the queue of people waiting to get on my boat disappeared faster than you could blink an eye."

Annie scanned the crowd in the direction her brothers had taken but they were nowhere to be seen. It wasn't the first time either herself or Jamie had been approached by Fergus to cover a debt and they been happy to help him in the past. In recent months his requests had become much more frequent and the couple had agreed not to continue supporting what they considered a bad habit.

"You did the right thing, Jamie," assured Annie, "Don't you worry about filling the boat.

Me and the girls, will have a line of people gathered for you in no time."

True to her word, Jamie's boat was filled and each time he came back to shore another handful of day-trippers stood waiting their turn. By the end of the day, Annie had a purse full of coins and treated the children to some sweets from one of the last remaining stalls, before heading back home. Jamie would not be too long behind her and she wanted to have a good supper on the table for him on his return.

Approaching her home, Annie wasn't surprised to see Fergus sitting on the windowsill, waiting for her. She had refused to lend him some money earlier and noticed him watching her from a distance, as she drummed up business for her husband. She suspected he might turn up at their home later in the day to try his luck again.

"I have already told you, we cannot give you any more money," Annie brushed past him before he could ask again.

Following her through the doorway, Fergus snatched the purse from her hands and poured some coins into his palm.

"Here you go, children. Off with you, now, and buy some sweeties for yourselves, for all the hard work you've done today helping to fill your da's boat."

Annie could see a dark menacing look on her brother's face and for the first time in her life she was afraid of what he might do. The children noticed it, too, and stood like statues, waiting to see how their mother would react.

"Your uncle is right, go and see if that stall is still there and get yourselves a few more sweeties," Annie smiled reassuringly at her children.

Seeing they were hesitant to leave, she gently pushed them towards the door, "Go on, now. Hurry along or they'll be gone. And fetch me a few of those bonbons, while you're at it."

Annie knew she would have to try and diffuse the situation before Jamie arrived home so she invited Fergus to stay for supper. Instead of answering her, he emptied the contents of her purse into his pockets and handed it back to her.

"I'm sorry, Annie, but I have to take it. I'll pay you back, I promise," his voice was full of shame and he couldn't look her in the eye.

"At least leave me half of it, that way Jamie might not come after you straight away. You're only asking for trouble from him if you don't," Annie pleaded.

Without a word of reply, her brother turned towards the door and bumped into Jamie.

"What's your hurry, Fergus? Are you not staying to eat with us? I know how much you love your sister's cooking."

The two men stood eye to eye, with Jamie blocking his brother-in-law's exit.

"You don't want your children to see us like this, do you? They could walk in any minute now," Fergus could feel his temper rise.

"They've gone with Da to Mary-Anne's for supper. Although I doubt they'll have room for any food after all the sweets they ate," Jamie replied icily.

Annie felt sick with the fear of what might happen next. This confrontation had been a long time coming and only for her husband's patience with her brother, it would have taken place a lot sooner.

"Let's all sit down and have a nice cup of tea," she suggested. "Or would you men prefer a wee drop of porter? I think I have some left over from that cake I made this morning. Now let me see, where did I put that bottle?" Annie was on her knees searching through the lower shelves of the kitchen dresser.

"I think you should join the children for supper at Mary-Anne's. I'll come and get you after myself and Fergus have sorted out our differences."

By the tone of his voice, Annie knew not to argue with her husband and squeezed past him to get through the door, glaring over his shoulder at Fergus as she did so.

"If Sergeant Broderick is there when you go up, will you send him down to us, Annie? He might be able to get your brother to see sense if I cannot."

Jamie noticed how tightly Fergus clenched his fists and knew it was at the mention of the sergeant. He waited until they were alone before speaking.

"I know yourself and the sergeant haven't seen eye to eye on much lately, so now might be a good time to clear the air, Fergus."

With a slump of his shoulders, Fergus released the tension in his body and stood like a broken man, shrunken in size, in the middle of the room.

Jamie immediately felt sorry for him and pulled a chair out from the table. "Come on now, sit yourself down and tell me how much trouble your gambling has gotten you into."

Lifting his head, Fergus put his two index fingers between his lips and stretched his mouth wide open. Jamie peered inside, not sure what he was supposed to be looking for.

"Did you see those gaps between my teeth? I didn't have them pulled, they were knocked out. There's nothing like a good thrashing to squeeze money out of a man, even when he thinks he has nothing left to give."

"I'm not the only one to have noticed the bruising on your face and arms of late," Jamie's voice was now much softer. "Would that be the work of Mallet Mulligan by any chance?"

Fergus nodded and bowed his head in shame. For a long time the men allowed the silence of the house to wrap itself around them, neither one having any desire to break it by speaking. Remorse and compassion replaced their earlier hostility towards one another, until a loud knock made them both jump. Not waiting for a response, Sergeant Broderick swung the door open and strode in, a dark scowl across his face.

When Jamie stood as if to leave the table, the sergeant shook his head and gestured for him to sit down. The silence between the three men only added to the tension.

Fergus shifted anxiously in his seat, "This is family business, Sergeant. There's no need for you to be here at all," he turned to face Jamie and gave a weak smile. "Sure there's no reason why we cannot sort this out ourselves. Isn't that right?"

Before Jamie could answer Sergeant Broderick cut in, "I'm not here to interfere in family business, Fergus. There's a much more serious matter that needs addressing and I think you know what it's about. Now, do the right thing and admit to what you've been up to?"

"I'm surprised by your concern over a bit of gambling, Sergeant. I'm not the first man in the village to have fallen on hard times over a wager, or to have asked one of his family for a loan," desperate to repair his wounded pride, Fergus straightened his shoulders and glared at both men.

The sergeant's patience was wearing thin, "I couldn't care less about your gambling, and if someone is foolish enough to give you a loan, that's their business. But when you put your comrades in danger for thirty pieces of silver, then it becomes my business."

Fergus gave his brother-in-law a puzzled look, "What's he talking about? I never asked anyone for any silver."

Jamie cleared his throat, "He means betrayal, Fergus. Like Judas did to Our Lord. You know, he took money in exchange for pointing him out."

"I know the gospel as well as any man, but what has that got to do with *me*. I never took any money for pointing anyone out, and don't you go accusing me of such a thing, Broderick. What gives you the right to stick your nose in where it doesn't belong?"

"I've been ordered to find out who is passing on information to the militia and believe me, if I could get out of this assignment I would. Nobody is above suspicion, not even my own son, so don't you go telling me I'm sticking my nose in where it doesn't belong."

"And what about yourself, Sergeant? Or are you above suspicion," Fergus smirked.

Before Jamie could stop him, Sergeant Broderick lashed out and slapped the smile off his brother-in-law's face. All three men jumped to their feet at the same time and Jamie pressed his palms into his companions' chests, struggling to keep them apart.

"Maybe we should take this outside, where we cannot do any damage to my sister's furniture," Fergus challenged.

"Ah, would you sit down, the two of ye, and stop acting like young fellas in a schoolyard."

Jamie's words seemed to hit home and Sergeant Broderick was the first to take his seat. Fergus nodded and did likewise, spreading his hands out on the table, palms down.

"Look, here's the honest truth, Sergeant. I've been letting the gambling get the better of me of late and got myself into a bit of trouble over it."

"He means trouble with Mallet Mulligan," Jamie explained.

The sergeant nodded and looked at the bruising on the hands stretched out on the table in front of him. Fergus noticed the attention they were receiving and folded them out of sight on his lap.

"I see you had an argument with a hammer, or some such implement," said the sergeant.

"Something like that," replied Fergus. "Look, if I was getting paid to inform would I be asking Mulligan for a loan?" his knuckles were beginning to throb at the reminder of what had been done to them.

"Well now, that might depend on how much debt you were in, Fergus," the sergeant's voice was calm and even, reflecting his demeanour. "Or how much pain."

Noting the set look on both men's faces, Jamie knew they would be in for a long night and suggested they carry on their discussion at Paddy Mac's. Sergeant Broderick was hesitant to bring attention to anyone until he was fully sure they were guilty of informing and Johnny Mac would know he suspected Fergus, if they were to bring him there. Fergus knew this too.

"Can we not go somewhere else? I swear to you on my . . . on my . . . grandmother's grave, I have never informed on anyone. I swear on my life I haven't."

The sergeant paced across the room, willing himself to give the anxious man the benefit of the doubt.

"I'm sorry, Fergus, but time is running out for both of us and if I don't show that I'm at least suspecting someone, this will be taken out of my hands," Sergeant Broderick almost weakened at the contrite look on the young man's face.

"Right so, I'd best be fetching my young ones home to bed, or do you need me to go with you?" James was directing the question as much to Fergus as he was to the sergeant.

"I don't think it will be necessary for the both of us to escort him to Paddy Mac's," Sergeant Broderick waited for a sign and was relieved to see a reluctant nod from Fergus.

"Well in that case, I'll be on my way," Jamie hated leaving but knew that he would not be welcome at such a meeting, on account of him being related by marriage to the suspect.

"Tell Mary-Anne not to wait up for me, will you, Jamie?"

Fergus visibly winced at the sergeant's words, he knew he was in for a long, disturbing night.

CHAPTER FOURTEEN

Frank McGrother learned a lot in the few days he had been in Carrickmacross, as a guest of his distant relatives, but one very important piece of knowledge still eluded him – the whereabouts of his paternal grandparents' grave. The blacksmith and his wife had been more than generous with their hospitality and even though they refused his offer of payment for lodging with them, they were grateful for the repairs around the house and forge, carried out by Frank during his stay. However, he was running out of time.

Some older men of the town had quickly become used to the young Australian sitting alongside them as they watched the comings and goings of their neighbours. They had even shared their personal stories with him and Frank could hear the pain in their voices as they recounted a litany of tragic events that made his blood boil.

Now and again, someone would pass them by and nod or shout out a greeting. This would elicit another sad account from the men about the person's relatives. It seemed to Frank that just about every family in the town had suffered in some way from starvation, eviction or emigration.

The years of blight from 1845 to 1848 destroyed potato harvests all over Europe. To prevent those who were starving in Ireland from eating crops, vegetables and animals intended for export by landlords for profit, the British Government increased its battalions there, by sending in another twenty thousand troops. This played a large part in the resulting Great Hunger, An Gorta Mór, and the starving poor, often sick with fever, begged for admission to the dreaded workhouses.

Carrickmacross workhouse was originally built to house five hundred people but by 1851, with Ireland having suffered years of famine, almost two thousand men, women and children had been packed into the building, including many orphans.

"I think my father would have left Ireland by choice, had he not being transported. Knowing the man he was, I cannot see him living in a place where there is so little hope of changing your fortune."

The two men sharing the bench with him looked at Frank for a moment before one of them spoke.

"But sure, was it not Australia that made him the man he was, son?"

This question hit the young man like a bucket of ice cold water and capped the anger seething within him. Ever since the parish priest uttered the words *shame* and *poor*, Frank had been struggling to control a rage that threatened to erupt at any given moment.

"Do you not think my father would have had his own land given half a chance, here in Ireland?" Frank was now trying to look at things from a different angle.

One of the older men shifted his position and brushed the dust from the street off his clothes, as if he was preparing to stand up and leave. He was, in fact, gathering his thoughts before making a reply. The anger and frustration that had been brewing in the young Australian was plain to see.

The older men of the town were well used to hearing about the lack of opportunity afforded the less fortunate in Irish society, from the mouths of their own sons and daughters. Had it not been the same for them, in their youth? Had they, themselves, not done plenty of complaining to their own parents? In the end, some of them left, following the trail of older siblings or cousins on a boat to another land with the prospect of a better life. Others remained and married, if they could afford to, channelling all of their youthful energy into the rearing of the next generation.

"Maybe your father would have gone to America and gotten himself one of them homesteads over there, if he had not been sent to Australia. If a desire for land is strong enough in a man's heart, he will find a way to own a piece of it, even if it means traveling to the other side of the world. Either way, son, you might never have been born here, on our wee island," the man looked sadly at his young companion.

Frank let out a long sigh, "I suppose you're right about that. But I know my father's last thoughts were about Ireland and the family he left behind here. How am I going to fulfil his wishes if I cannot find their resting place?"

The old men sucked on well-worn clay pipes, while contemplating their companion's predicament but no one came up with a solution. Frank inhaled the familiar smell of tobacco that always hung about his father, savouring the memories it triggered. He touched the breast pocket of his jacket, where he carried the pouch containing the lock of his father's hair, and surveyed the wide main street.

Frank experienced a measure of consolation, knowing he was in a place where his missing relatives once stood. His father's eyes would have rested upon the same scene on his visits to the town on market day and he may have been seated with friends in the same spot, discussing their chances of attracting the attention of the young women passing by. Even if he never found his grandparents' grave, it was worth the long journey he had made, to sit there among his father's people and sample a small part of his life.

Half the town, at this stage, had been told of the young Australian's search for his grandparent's grave. It meant a lot to Frank that so many strangers would put themselves out to help him in his task, even sending messages to friends and relatives in other parishes to check the headstones in their local cemeteries.

"Well, gentlemen, I must be getting back to my lodgings. I promised young Mattie I would take his place working the bellows for his father at the forge, so he could go off and do a bit of fishing. I'll call at the priests' house on the way," Frank stood and stretched his legs, "You never know, one of them might have a bit of good news for me today."

The men waved him off and wished him luck at the parochial house, telling him not to give up hope. Inwardly, each one felt that his search would be fruitless but no one had the heart to tell him.

The following morning one of the priests put an end to any hope Frank had of finding his grandparents' resting place – there had been no positive news from the surrounding churches. The search was becoming futile and the few relatives in England Frank already knew of, had less information than he did about departed family members in Ireland. With years of hunger, strife and little to show for whatever work they could find, driving them from their homeland, who could blame anyone for putting the past behind them and looking only to the future?

It seemed to the young man that his ancestors had been wiped out in just a few years and their descendants scattered to the four corners of the earth. There was no way of knowing for sure if his father's parents had ended their days in the workhouse but Frank resigned himself to the fact that it was most likely the case. On his last day in Carrickmacross, with a sad reluctance that took him a little by surprise, the young Australian said his goodbyes to the family he had stayed with and the old men of the town who had made him feel so close to his father, with their similar accents and turn of phrase.

Frank's last stop before catching the train was a visit to the workhouse. The parish priest had made arrangements for him to be shown the area where his grandparents might have been interred. Most of the unfortunate people dying in the workhouse during the famine years had been buried there, some of their names not even listed in the records. As his eyes swept sadly over the large patches of grass covering the mass graves, Frank's hand went up to the pocket holding the lock of his father's hair.

The large stone wall young Mattie had pointed out to him, while searching for his grandparents' house, came to mind. Frustration turned to anger at the owners of a structure that most likely contained the home his father grew up in. It became an ugly symbol of division to the young Australian, separating not just the land but the people, too, and an uncharacteristic revulsion towards the gentry took hold of him.

"I'll wager they have their own graves well marked," Frank said bitterly.

He quickly looked around to see if anyone had heard his remark but the caretaker who had brought him to the rear of the workhouse was nowhere to be seen. Ireland was having a strange effect on the young man and the longer he stayed, the more resentful he could see himself becoming. Frank knew his father would not have wanted him to feel such rage, nor to take it back to Australia with him and infect his brothers with it.

By sending his son to his native land, Francis McGrother would have been hoping any family still there would welcome him with open arms, as if it was himself that had returned. He would have been pleased to see, not only his relatives, but the people of Carrickmacross, too, extend such warmth to the young Australian.

Frank had intended picking a spot in one of the mass burial sites in which to bury the lock of his father's hair but standing now in such a cold, anonymous place, he changed his mind. Praying did not usually come easy to him but he paid his respects to all who were buried there, whether they were related to him or not.

A thought suddenly struck him and it became as clear as day what he should do to honour his father's dying wish. This was not the place to do that and Frank's spirits lifted as he turned on his heel and almost ran to the station, to wait for his train to Dundalk. Now that he knew what he should do, the young man was impatient to finish the task he had taken on, so many months before, on the other side of the world.

When he boarded the train, Frank chose a seat by the window and thought of home and his family's vast tracts of open grassland. It was very different to the wooded hills of Monaghan and the surrounding patchwork of fields, separated by hedges and old stone walls. What a shock Australia must have been to his father, just as this landscape seemed so alien to him. But it wasn't the foreign scenery that made him feel homesick, it was the closed in sensation, threatening to smother him everywhere he went.

Frank was used to the wide open spaces of his family's ranch. Although the physical features played a part in making him feel almost claustrophobic, it was the lack of opportunity and an air of oppression that bothered him most. His father had taken advantage of the chance to improve his circumstances, even though he had arrived in Australia as a convict. The likelihood of that ever happening in Ireland would have been very remote, especially with a prison record to tarnish your reputation. With most of the land in the possession of gentry, Frank concluded that his own life and that of his brothers would have been very different had his father remained in his native land.

Yet it was to this hard pressed little island his father's last thoughts had turned and Frank would never have understood why, had he not made this journey. The memory of his people had drawn Francis McGrother's heart back to the land of his youth, like an invisible umbilical cord that had never been completely severed.

CHAPTER FIFTEEN

Annie had been unable to sleep, knowing her brother was being interrogated at Paddy Mac's. Fergus, an informer? How could her husband, Jamie, even think that he would do such a thing? The more she brooded over it the more she felt the need to do something and before she knew it, Annie was on her way to her parents' farm, in the middle of a very dark night. Dark in more ways than just a lack of moonlight, concern for her brother distracting her from the fact that she was out on the road alone at such a late hour.

Whispering a name as she approached the house, Annie was greeted by the thud of a wagging tale from the large kennel where her father's sheep dog, a black and white border collie, slept. Although a good worker out in the fields, he was lazy around the farm and loved his bed, only leaving it to bark out a warning, should a stranger approach.

At night, the kennel door was closed and Annie spoke softly to the dog as she slowly eased back the squeaking bolt securing the door. By this time, the thudding tail was making more noise than the rusted metal, especially when Annie leaned into the large wooden structure to scratch behind the dog's ears. But it wasn't too long before she had soothed him back to sleep.

Anxious to avoid alerting the rest of the family to the trouble Fergus was in, Annie threw stones at the window of the bedroom he shared with his youngest brother. When it finally creaked open, the young man was shocked to see his sister at such a late hour standing alone on the grass below.

"Come down and let me in, Brian, and mind you don't make a sound."

Once inside the warm kitchen, Annie questioned her brother about Fergus's gambling and asked if he knew that money had been borrowed from Mallet Mulligan.

Brian nodded his head, knowing it would be pointless lying to his sister, she would see right through it.

"He's been trying to pay it back for a while now, Annie, but Mulligan kept adding more and more interest to it until it looked like the loan was never going to be paid off. And the beatings were getting worse, too."

When his sister told him Fergus was in Paddy Mac's, being interrogated by Johnny Mac and Sergeant Broderick, over passing on information, Brian began to pace the floor, muttering to himself.

"Shhhh. You'll have the whole house awake," scolded Annie. "There's no need to worry the rest of the family about this, I'm sure it's all a big mistake. I'll never believe our Fergus would turn informer, not for any amount of money."

Brian stopped in his tracks, "He didn't. It was me. Oh, Annie, what have I done? I was only trying to help."

For a moment, Annie was frozen to the chair she was sitting on, unable to process what had been said, but it didn't take long for the gravity of the situation to sink in.

"Why didn't you come to me about this, or tell Da? I know he would have beaten the living daylights out of Fergus but at least that's better than Mallet Mulligan doing it."

"I couldn't, Annie. Fergus had already borrowed from everyone in the family. Da told him not to ask for another farthing and warned him to stay away from you and Jamie. I thought the first time I spoke to the militia would be the last but Mulligan said there was interest to be paid, and Fergus just kept placing more wagers in the hopes of getting a big win and clearing his debts."

"And he doesn't know a thing about what you've been doing. Is that right, Brian?" asked Annie.

Her brother shook his head, "Fergus would have killed me if he found out what I was up to."

Annie sighed and put an arm around the young man, "He won't have to kill you, there's others will be only too willing to do that, Brian. You know what happens to informers, don't you?"

Nodding his head as he reached for his jacket, Brian told his sister he would have to go to Paddy Mac's straight away and face the consequences. He couldn't let Fergus suffer through the night for something he hadn't done.

"He's as much to blame as you, Brian. If it wasn't for his gambling, neither of you would be in this sorry mess," Annie waited by the door while her brother put his boots on. "We had better walk back, the noise of the cart would wake up Da or set the dog barking."

Before facing the music at Paddy Mac's, Brian walked Annie to her door, where she embraced him for a long time before sending

111

him on his way. They parted company without speaking a word. As the stove had been packed up with turf earlier in the night, the heat of her kitchen enveloped her chilled body as soon as she stepped through the door. Although she would have preferred to stay longer in the warmest room in the house, Annie knew better than to tempt fate. She was thankful everyone was still asleep and her absence at such a late hour had not been noticed.

Tiptoeing up the narrow stairs, she quickly undressed and slipped back under the bed covers, praying her cold feet would not disturb her husband. If he woke up she would tell him that sleep had evaded her and she had spent the past few hours sitting in the parlour, worrying about Fergus. It would only be half a lie.

Two days later, Fergus and his younger brother, Brian, found themselves standing in the middle of their kitchen, crying almost as much as their mother and sisters as they kissed them goodbye. The rest of the boys in their family had wives and children, and lived in another parish. Fergus and Brian had been warned by Johnny Mac not to bid any farewells to their married brothers, nor let them know anything about their exile. They could not risk them interfering, it would only make things worse for everyone concerned.

Rigid as a statue, their father stood to one side, watching the heart-breaking scene. His usually tanned face, pale and tight with unexpressed emotion. He didn't know whether to strike his sons or embrace them along with his wife and daughters, he was so filled with painful rage.

The young men were not sure if they should take a step closer to the man who had played such a big part in their lives, whose eyes seemed to be burning into their bones. It was Annie who reached out to her father and pulled him into their grief-stricken circle.

Jamie looked through the open doorway at a scene he had witnessed too many times in his own family, but for his in-laws it was even more upsetting. Australia was so far away, everyone knew there was practically no hope of seeing one another again. If all went according to plan, Fergus and Brian would set sail from Liverpool to a land that could offer them a fresh start.

Johnny Mac had come up with the idea in the hopes of sparing Brian's life. Even America would have been too near to ensure the young man's safety. At first, Annie's brothers protested that it was too far from home, until Johnny Mac reminded them of the large network supporting the cause in the United States. He said Brian might as well hide out in England, for all the good it would do. Being exiled to Australia might be considered a fair enough punishment. Sergeant Broderick made a sarcastic remark about the Irish now transporting their own, while the English no longer carried out such a punishment.

Fergus could not bear to think of his younger brother being sent to a land so far from everyone he knew and loved, and insisted he go with him. At first, Brian refused to have Fergus suffer the same fate but it didn't take much convincing to change his mind. Whatever chance he had of making a go of it in America, where many of his friends and neighbours had already settled, he could not face being alone in Australia.

Being part of a close knit family, Brian and Fergus knew it would break their mother's heart to suddenly lose two of her children, having managed so far to keep them all together but their father's reaction took them all by surprise. He broke free from the weeping circle and dragged his sons outside, almost knocking Jamie over in the process.

The men watched their father bend down and pick up a handful of earth. With tears glistening in his eyes, he placed some of it in each of their palms and squeezed them shut.

"Never forget where ye come from, boys" were the last words he spoke to his eldest and youngest sons.

The plan was to send them to where Frank McGrother's family might be in a position to offer them some work, at least until the young men found their feet. As everything had happened so quickly, this had not yet been discussed with the Australian visitor but Sergeant Broderick was sure he would help them, if it was within his power to do so. If not, making their way alone in a distant land was still better than the alternative.

Jamie and Annie brought her brothers to the quayside in Dundalk. As they jumped from the back of the cart he helped his wife down from where she had been seated beside him on the solemn journey to town.

"Be strong now, love. For Brian's sake," Jamie whispered. "The poor lad is barely holding himself together."

Annie nodded and wiped her eyes before turning around. Her brothers smiled bravely and kissed her cheeks, assuring her they would see her again in the future. In spite of the fact that nobody believed it, the words were enough to prevent the flood of tears she was struggling to hold back.

"I know the two of ye will land on your feet, especially yourself, Fergus. If you fell into a dung heap you'd stand up smelling of roses, wouldn't you?"

"Aye, I would at that, Annie. Let's hope our luck stays that way."

"Of course it will, Fergus," said Jamie. "Sure look how it turned out for my father's cousin."

The words were meant to have a positive effect but Annie burst into tears. "He never stepped foot on Irish soil again," she cried.

It was useless to try and conceal the depth of her grief any longer and the two brothers could only pat their sister consolingly on the back as she wept into the shirt on her husband's chest. Jamie was afraid to take his arms from around her for fear she might fall to the ground.

"Sure wasn't I made for the hot weather they have there, Annie? It'll warm up these cold Irish bones of mine," Fergus slapped his fair skinned younger brother on the back. "It's a good thing I'm so much taller than you, Brian. You can hide from the sun in my shadow."

The young man gave a weak laugh, eager to cheer his sister up. "I will indeed and I daresay I'll need to. I'll be as red as one of Ma's strawberries after a day's work in an Australian field."

Incapable of looking at her brothers, Annie shook her head and buried it deeper into her husband's shirt. The men gave each other awkward glances and waited patiently until the racking sobs became soft whimpers, before bidding a final farewell.

As they watched Fergus and Brian board the boat for Liverpool, Jamie held Annie tightly in his arms. Earlier that morning he made her a promise he knew in his heart he would never be able to keep. He was far too involved in the cause to leave it now but knew she needed to hear him say the words, even if they were untrue.

CHAPTER SIXTEEN

As they sat on the grassy bank of the River Fane, watching cattle graze in a field on the other side of the fast flowing water, Frank asked James if he had ever been tempted to steal food during the famine years.

"I was and I did," came the reply.

Frank waited but nothing more was said. He didn't want to pry so allowed his gaze to follow the river's current as it rushed towards the sea. Eventually, curiosity got the better of the young man.

"I take it you were never caught, or you might have joined my father in Australia."

James tapped his old clay pipe against the palm of his hand and scattered tobacco ash across the grass. "No, I was never caught," he said.

While the pipe was being refilled, Frank thought about the significance of what they were discussing. He wondered if James had been with his father when he stole the cow that resulted in him being transported as a convict. As if reading his mind, James gave an explanation.

"I would never risk what your father did, Frank. The penalty was too high a price for me to pay. But there was many a hungry mouth grateful to him for what he did, my own included."

"Did you poach rabbits?" asked Frank. "The men I made friends with in Carrickmacross told me they did so, themselves. I can't blame them, sure wild animals don't belong to anyone, do they?"

"No, son, they don't. But if the land is private, then you're trespassing and if you catch a fish or a rabbit on it, you're poaching. Some years back, a woman from Blackrock was up in petty sessions for gathering spring nettles on a private estate."

"But they are just weeds, are they not? Why would that bother anyone?" Frank was genuinely confused. "I should think they'd be happy to have their garden cleared of them."

"That's just the way of it, son," sighed James.

The sound of the river intensified in the silence that followed and both men continued to stare at the cattle on the other side.

"Do you see how those cows over yonder are flicking away the flies with their tails?" James pointed his pipe in their direction.

Frank nodded, adding that all cows do it, even Australian ones.

"Aye, they do indeed. But there were quite a few cows and a bull or two during the hungry years that had no tail to flick. Tormented by flies they were, the poor creatures," James frowned at the recollection of an old memory.

"Are you telling me you stole a tail from a cow?"

"I did, Frank. I never bled a cow but there were many who did, to strengthen their starving children during those bad years. It never did the animal any harm, not that I know of," James sucked on his pipe for a moment while his mind travelled back more than half a century.

"Was it your own cow?"

"Not at all," replied James. "Our cow was sold months before that. We were short of food after the potato crop failed. The landlord was looking for stones to build another stable as the one he had was too small for his collection of pedigree horses, so we sold the walls of our byre to him. It bought us some bags of oats and a few month's rent. But come winter the weather was very harsh and we had nowhere to shelter our cow. The few hens we had left uneaten we kept in the house with us at night, as was the custom in those days, but Mary drew the line at bringing a cow inside."

"I can't say as I blame her, James," said Frank.

"So we sold the cow to keep a roof over our heads. That's what we all feared more than hunger, son, losing our homes. Especially when there's children to care for."

The young Australian could only imagine how daunting it must have been, facing a cold, damp Irish winter and nowhere to shelter your family. He pulled his jacket closed and shivered at the thought.

"Did it recover?" asked Frank.

"Did what recover?" James had lost track of the conversation, having gone so far back into his past.

"The cow, the one you took the tail from."

"Of course it did. Sure I knew how to take a pup's tail without causing the animal any serious harm. No difference with a cow, except there's more of it," the older man smiled at his next memory. "I got Mary to cook it and made her swear to her mother that it was a hare. But I knew she wasn't fooled, she must have known what it was by the taste. She never said a word, though, just smiled when her children's faces lit up at their first decent meal in weeks."

Both men sat in quiet contemplation, allowing the urgent sound of the water fill the emptiness settling between them. Frank watched a small branch being tossed and turned as it was carried towards the mouth of the river, reminding himself that soon he would be following the same route on a long journey home to the other side of the world.

"I suppose you'll be heading off any day now, will you, son?" it was as if James had read his thoughts.

"I've been thinking about it, sure enough," was the reply.

"And have you decided what to do with that lock of hair you've been carrying around with you?"

Frank nodded, "I have indeed. If it would be alright with you, I'd like to leave it here in the parish."

The young man watched the tobacco glow as his father's cousin sucked on the pipe's mouthpiece. He hoped that what he was about to ask would not cause offence, but having come to know James McGrother, he was sure his request would not be refused.

"And where have you decided to place it, Frank?"

"Do we still have some time to spare before going to Mary-Anne's for our midday meal?"

The old fisherman looked at the sun's position in the sky before nodding his head. "Help me up off this damp grass, I'm not as quick at standing up as I am at sitting down. As long as we don't have to walk to Dundalk and back, we should have enough time."

"It's not too far. Besides, I would like to pay my respects to your good wife before I leave for Liverpool."

James gave his young companion a puzzled look, "Is it with myself and Mary you want to place that lock of hair?"

"It is, but I will understand if you think that's not a suitable place to leave it," Frank wasn't sure what he would do should he get a negative response.

As they walked through the village, returning salutes and greetings from neighbours, James pondered over the prospect of his own grave being a symbolic resting place for his cousin and childhood friend. It wasn't even in the same county, so would it truly fulfil Francis McGrother's dying wish?

"The last time your father was in Blackrock he was seasick. Do you not think he would object to being laid to rest, so to speak, in a place that held such memories for him? Would he not have preferred anywhere in Monaghan rather than by the sea, and in a different county, at that?"

By the time Frank had given this some serious thought, Haggardstown cemetery was just yards ahead and James was beginning to think the young man was having a change of heart.

"I took it for granted that there would at least be a ruin of some sort marking the whereabouts of my father's house. It wouldn't feel right to leave a lock of his hair just anywhere as long as it's in Monaghan. It was the connection to family that meant more to him, James."

The old fisherman understood the sentiment behind the request and assured his young relative that Mary would not have objected to her grave being chosen for Francis McGrother's lock of silver hair. James removed his cap and asked Frank to wait by the entrance for a few minutes while he paid his respects to his wife in private.

The short walk to the plot where he himself would be laid to rest one day took James past the grave that held his Uncle Pat and Aunt Annie. His sister Maggie had also been laid to rest with them and he made the sign of a cross over his heart, silently promising a longer visit next time.

As was his custom, James stood to one side of his wife's grave and placed a hand over the words etched into the headstone as he whispered a quick prayer. His long fingers easily covered the four letters of her name and he was reminded of the many times Mary's small hand had been enveloped by his own, especially during her final weeks.

Looking around the cemetery, James wondered how such a place could feel so peaceful, considering the sorrow and loss essentially bound to it.

"Well, my love, I have something to ask you," he spoke softly. "Do you remember my cousin, Francis McGrother, who robbed a cow and got himself transported for his trouble? Well, his youngest son, his namesake, would like to leave a lock of his father's hair in beside you, in our grave," James looked around to make sure he wasn't being overheard.

"Frank – that's what he calls himself – Frank has come all the way from Australia to fulfil my cousin's dying wish, only there wasn't a trace of his family home when we went to look for it in Monaghan. So here, with us, is the next best place. I know you won't object, Mary. It should be me who resents it, shouldn't it?" James smiled wryly.

When they were children James and Francis had been the best of friends, willing to share everything but one thing – the attention of Mary Roarke. For a long time, he was convinced that it was his cousin's company she preferred but in the end, it was James who won her heart, long before Francis was forced to leave them.

James cleared his throat and stepped back from the grave, "I knew you wouldn't mind, Mary. I'll go, now, and send him in. The poor lad will be anxious to finally carry out his task, after all these months. I'll come and visit you next week, love."

Having kissed his palm, he placed it once again over Mary's name before turning to make his way out of the cemetery.

CHAPTER SEVENTEEN

Coney Island was teeming with day-trippers, in spite of it being midweek. Patrick put a hand out to steady his bicycle as a crowd of boisterous young men rushed past the bench it was resting against. He turned to Jeremiah and saw he had done the same with his. A picnic Lily had prepared that morning lay on the slatted wooden seat between them, where they had stopped to take in the sea view.

"Where have they all come from?" asked Patrick. "Is there nobody at work or school today?"

Catherine's business had grown steadily over the years and the increased earnings from dressmaking allowed Patrick to reduce his own working week to just four days, at her insistence. Instead of being bored with more time on his hands, as he anticipated, Patrick was grateful to his wife for helping to make his life so much easier.

"Schools and colleges are closed, Uncle Patrick, but businesses are still open," Jeremiah pointed his cheese and chutney sandwich at the crowded beach. "I imagine a lot of them are teachers and professors, enjoying the few days off in the sunshine."

Patrick's hand shot out to steady his bicycle once more, as a group of young cyclists whizzed past them at a reckless speed in a pedestrian area.

"And their pupils, too, by the looks of it," he grumbled. "Sure of course the schools are shut, isn't that why you had the day free yourself?"

124

Patrick shook his head. "For someone who can recite an hour long speech from memory, I have a head like a sieve when it comes to everything else."

"Does that mean you cannot recall if it was my mother who suggested you invite me on this bicycle ride?" Jeremiah studied his uncle's face.

"I won't lie to you, son. She's been worried sick about you, ever since your father passed away."

Jeremiah smacked a hand off his knee, "I knew it. I just knew it. Why must she keep interfering in my life? Did she not say on more than one occasion that I am now the man of the house?"

"She did indeed. Sure I heard her myself when you gave me the bicycle. Didn't I ask her if she minded? After all, it belonged to her husband. And that's exactly what she said; *'I shall let my son decide. He's the man of the house, now.'* Those were her very words, as true as I'm sitting here on this bench."

Patrick's reminder had the intended calming effect on his nephew and it served to put both of them on the same side in Jeremiah's eyes.

"Exactly, so why am I constantly battling with her about my interest in Irish affairs?"

A seagull perched on a nearby railing eyed Patrick's sandwich with such a begging look, he couldn't resist breaking off a piece of bread and throwing it to the cheeky bird. Jeremiah looked around nervously, expecting an onslaught of feathered scavengers to appear.

"Please don't scatter any more bread about, Uncle Patrick. His friends might start flying about our heads, looking for more," the young man had been feeding pigeons in Central Park as a child and panicked when a great flock of them swooped over his head.

"Oh, I'm sorry, Jeremiah, that was thoughtless of me. I forgot you don't like birds."

"I'm fine as long as there's not too many of them."

Patrick realized he could use the situation to help his nephew understand his mother's fears.

"Do you feel like history is repeating itself, when you see a flock of birds, son? Does it bring back the same fear that you felt with those pigeons in the park?"

Having given the question some thought, Jeremiah acknowledged it was most likely the case.

"I suppose your mother feels the same way, every time she finds out that you've been to one of your meetings or rallies. It must bring her back to the last time she saw your father, the day he lost his life in that riot, rest his poor soul," Patrick sighed and blessed himself, to heighten the emotion.

Neither man made eye contact but continued to watch the seagull as it cocked its head to one side, returning their gaze.

"I know what you're doing, Uncle Patrick, and it won't work. In spite of my mother's fears, I shall continue to support what I believe in. I'm sure that in time she'll get used to it."

Having had enough of the feathered beggar and the subtle lecture, Jeremiah stood and took his bicycle by the handlebars. It was a clear signal the conversation had ended and Patrick mirrored his nephew's actions.

"Please tell my mother she has nothing to fear. I have decided to go into politics, I'm not sure where it will lead me but I want to make a difference in this world."

Slapping his nephew on the back, Patrick gave a whoop of joy, "Why on earth did you not tell us before now. Your poor mother was convinced that someday soon you'd be on a boat to Ireland, pistols blazing for the cause."

"I've been thinking about it for a long time now. Listening to the speeches you made about social change must have rubbed off on me, Uncle Patrick."

Watching the young man confidently mount his bicycle as if it was a stallion, Patrick had the strongest feeling he was in the presence of someone who would indeed make a difference.

CHAPTER EIGHTEEN

Having said a poignant goodbye to Frank, James took his grandchildren to sit on the wall in the main street of Blackrock. It was a place where he had done a great deal of thinking over the years, watching the ebb and flow of the sea. The children giggled as they teased the waves of a high tide, lapping at their dangling feet. Seagulls swooped across the water, squabbling over landing spaces, and James felt envious of their ability to float contentedly while he had need of a boat to do the same thing. Like himself, not many fishermen could swim and James was thankful to his son-in-law, Patrick Gallagher, for teaching his youngest when he was a child. Jamie, in turn, taught his own children to swim, and many of their friends, too.

James had been doing a lot of reminiscing of late, more so than was usual for him. He wondered if it was merely due to his Australian relative's visit and all the talk of the past, or was he nearing the end? The thought was not alarming to him, although, if he shared it with his son, Jamie, he knew what the reaction would be.

Whenever James pondered his own demise, it was his youngest son he fretted over. Not because he cared for him more than the rest of his children, he loved each of them equally, but he knew that Jamie would miss him the most. They had been constant companions for all of the young man's life and fished together for almost as long. James smiled as he remembered the nickname, Barnacle, his wife had given their youngest, as he was always to be found at his father's side.

An unusual thought came into James's head and he couldn't, for the life of him, shake it free. The old fisherman's eyes swept across the horizon as he considered asking Jamie to throw a lock of his hair into the sea, far out in the bay, after he had passed. A symbolic resting place, like the dying wish of his cousin Francis. The more he thought about it, the more determined he became and James made his mind up there and then to write it in a letter to Jamie.

As soon as he was back at the house, he would cut a lock of his own hair and put it in with the letter, to be opened after his funeral. In fact, he would write letters to all of his children, and grandchildren. James put a hand up to his thinning, silver crown, *'I can only spare one lock of hair, or I'll be as bald as a coot,'* he mused, smiling at his foolish notions. He could almost hear Mary tutting behind him until a persistent tugging at the sleeve of his jacket brought him back to his senses.

One of the children was pointing to a vessel on the horizon, "Is that the boat Cousin Frank is sailing to England on?"

"No, no. I think it will be a wee bit longer before his boat leaves the dock. That one looks too small to be a steam packet," James replied, squinting his eyes.

"Did you not want to say goodbye at the quayside in Dundalk, Granda?" asked the eldest girl.

"Ah, I've bid one too many farewells there, love. Besides, it's nice for your parents to spend a bit of time together, without you lot mithering them."

"What's mithering, Granda?"

James ruffled his youngest grandson's hair, "Asking too many questions, lad."

Ignoring the remark, the children begged their grandfather to tell them one of his stories but he pretended not to hear them, while quickly thinking of one. The high tide had drawn out some boats, barely dry from the previous night's fishing. James knew their crews would be tired and most likely taking turns catching forty winks. For a moment, he wished he was ten years younger and out in the bay alongside them. But the yearning was fleeting and his attention returned once again to his own crew of grandchildren, waiting patiently for his response.

"I have a new story, a very important one. Will ye promise to remember it long after I'm gone?"

He smiled at the row of eager, nodding heads, two of them the colour of the pale rushes adorning the wetlands at the south end of the village. The others with hair as dark as the wet turf, footed and drying in the bog.

"Where are you going, Granda? Can I come with you?" a little hand wove its way into his.

Pulling the toddler up onto his lap, James assured him he wasn't going anywhere just yet.

"Ye must tell this story to your own children and grandchildren, and make them promise to pass it on to their children and grandchildren. Will ye do this for me?"

The young heads nodded vigorously, anticipating a very special tale.

"Right, so. Now listen well. This story is about a poor young Irish lad who fed his whole village with a stolen cow and ended up owning a great big herd of cattle himself, on the other side of the world, no less."

"Is this one from the hungry years, Granda? Will it be a sad story?"

James smiled and patted the eldest girl's head, "It is, child, it is indeed. It's one of the saddest stories I've ever told. But it has a pleasant enough ending."

THE END

References

Chapter Eleven

The Earl Grey Scheme.
'Due to the large numbers of children in Workhouses, many of whom were orphaned by The Great Hunger, the English Government's Secretary of State for the Colonies, Earl Grey, devised the Pauper's Emigration Scheme. Under this scheme, between 1848 and 1850, 4,114 girls between the ages of 14 and 18 were emigrated from Irish Workhouses to Australia as wives and servants of the settlers and convicts there.'

This number included 38 girls from Carrickmacross Workhouse:

* 14 sailed on the 'Roman Emperor' to Adelaide

* 24 sailed on the 'John Knox' to Sydney.

http://www.irishfaminememorial.org/history /earl-grey-scheme/

http://www.carrickmacrossworkhouse.com/i ndex.php/history-of-workhouse

Estate Agent Mitchell
'Sandy Mitchell was the agent between 1829 and 1843 and has been described as the most tyrannical estate agent that the people of Farney had ever known. One taking up the appointment, he surveyed the estate and increased rents by as much as 30 per cent. He even imposed a rent

of between £4 and £8 per acre for bog land that had been free since time immemorial.

Mitchell died of apoplexy while attending the Spring Assizes in Monaghan in 1843. When the news of his 'sad parting' spread, bonfires were lit on every hilltop to celebrate the death of the "unscrupulous monster".'

http://www.irishidentity.com/stories/shirley
.htm

Author Bio

Jean Reinhardt was born in Louth, grew up in Dublin and lived in Alicante, Spain for almost eight years. With five children and five grandchildren, life is never dull. Now living in Ireland, she loves to read, write, listen to music and spend time with family and friends. When Jean isn't writing she likes to take long walks through the woods and on the beach. She writes poetry, short stories and novels and her favourite genres are Young Adult and Historical Fiction.

Follow her on:
www.twitter.com/JeanReinhardt1

Like her on:
www.facebook.com/JeanReinhardtWriter

Join her on:
www.jeanreinhardt.wordpress.com

Other books by the author:

An Irish Family Saga: a series of historical fiction novellas.

A Pocket Full of Shells (Book 1)
A Year of Broken Promises (Book 2)
A Turning of the Tide (Book 3)
A Legacy of Secrets (Book 4)
A Prodigal Return (Book 5)
A Time to Make Amends (Book 6)

The Finding Trilogy: a young adult medical thriller.

Book 1: Finding Kaden
Book 2: Finding Megan
Book 3: Finding Henry Brubaker

All books are in digital format on Amazon and Smashwords. Some are available as audio books. Paperbacks can be ordered from Amazon, The Book Depository and Createspace.

Acknowledgements

As always I'm extremely grateful to my Beta Readers for taking on the early drafts and giving me their honest feedback; Brenda, Joyce, Eileen, Alan, Peter, Carol, Motoko and Elaine.

Many thanks to Noel Sharkey (historian and poet)

The following books proved to be a great source of information in the writing of this story. They are full of well documented events and photographs of people whose families have lived in Blackrock for many generations, including my own:

The Parish of Haggardstown & Blackrock – A History by Noel Sharkey.
First Printed in 2003 by Dundalgan Press (W. Tempest) Ltd., Dundalk.

The Parish of Haggardstown & Blackrock – A Pictorial Record
Compiled and written by Noel Sharkey with photos by Owen Byrne.
Printed in 2008 by Dundalgan Press (W. Tempest) Ltd., Dundalk.

5963

Made in the USA
Middletown, DE
16 August 2018